WILLARD MEMORIAL LIBRARY
WILLARD, OH

1. Books may be kept two weeks and may be renewed twice for the same period except reserve and 7 day books.
2. A fine is charged for each day a book is not returned according to the above rule. No book will be issued to any person incurring such a fine until it has been paid.
3. All damages to books beyond reasonable wear and all losses shall be made good to the satisfaction of the Librarian.
4. Each borrower is held responsible for all books drawn on his card and for all fines accuring on the same.

LARGE PRINT   DEMCO

TREASURE TRAIL FROM TUCSON

Nelson Nye

Charlie Medders was riled. He had been prospecting for close to ten years, living from hand to mouth under the Arizona sun, without a bit of luck to sink his teeth into. Now, at last, he had a strike, the richest damned silver ore anybody had ever seen.

But, Tiberius Jones the banker who already owned most everything worth having in these parts, had got himself a court order taking the mine away from Charlie.

Tiberius Jones was shortly to learn that there's nothing more stubborn and cantankerous than a hard-bitten prospector with his back up.

Other Large Print Books
by Nelson Nye

MAVERICK MARSHALL

NELSON NYE

Treasure Trail From Tucson

John Curley & Associates, Inc.
South Yarmouth, Ma.

Library of Congress Cataloging-in-Publication Data

Nye, Nelson C. (Nelson Coral), 1907–
  Treasure trail from Tucson.

  1. Large type books.   I. Title.
  [PS3527.Y33T74   1988]   813'.54   88–16169
  ISBN 1-55504-686-X (lg. print)
  ISBN 1-55504-667-3 (pbk. : lg. print)

Published in Large Print by arrangement with Berkley Publishing Group for the United States and Canada, the U.K. and British Commonwealth L.P. Rights.

Distributed in Great Britain, Ireland and the Commonwealth by CHIVERS BOOK SALES LIMITED, Bath BA1 3HB, England.

Printed in Great Britain

Treasure Trail From Tucson

I

She was a sorry looking sight, no two ways about it.

Teetered back in his swivel Sheriff Andy McFarron continued with increasing irritation to stare. The yarn she'd come up with seemed about as unlikely as playing a harp with a hammer and, while he did not personally care for any part of it, certain aspects of it were going to have to be looked into. Banker Jones, anyway, could be relied on to think so.

Irascibly the sheriff blew the drip off his nose.

The dingy room was thick with trapped heat. This was Tucson in the belly of July and the range lay parched as buzzard picked bones. Hell was the only hotter place a man could picture. The forlorn bawling of gaunted cattle filled the midmorning quiet, monotonous and oppressive as the notions clambering through McFarron's head. "How long you been out there?"

The girl licked at cracked lips. "It was always night," she said, belligerent. She

1

couldn't have looked much worse if she'd been hauled through a knot hole. Yet back of her bangles, the torn, stained tawdry rags of an itinerant gypsy, she was shapely, emotional, cramjammed with passion. But her eyes were too watchful.

There had to be more to this deal than she'd told. The seething resentment boiling out of each gesture had to have more basis than was so far apparent. Not that her yarn wasn't loco enough! Cougar wild it was – you might's well say downright preposterous, and yet. . . .

McFarron, grimacing, pushed a hand through damp hair.

This wasn't like Charlie; but deep inside he could see the fool doing it. They had known each other clean back to the days they had both punched cows for John Slaughter. Even then Charlie Medders had been a "character". Nothing had been too reckless for him, and nothing McFarron had heard about him since held out any hope his temper had changed much.

Man ought to stretch a few points for old times' sake and, had it been anyone else, McFarron probably would have but – politics being what they were around here – he was caught in a bind. Tiberius K. Jones, local arbiter of destiny, was after Medders' scalp and the sheriff, with elections coming on, had to keep his fences up.

He considered the girl again, trying to make her claims fit the man she was accusing, and growled under his breath. All his life Charlie'd shied away from women, and this was the bone McFarron couldn't shake. He said, leaning forward: "You sure it was Medders?"

You could see it put her hackles up.

McFarron saw, but went on to speak anyway. "Mebbe you better describe him," he said but, time she got done, there was no possibility of it being someone else. She had old Charlie right under the nether millstone.

Though he'd taken her over the story three times McFarron couldn't faze her, couldn't even begin to. She had it down letter perfect, and if she ever got into a court with this yarn cold winters wasn't going to bother Charlie any more.

Beneath those brush clawed tatters she was hard as nails. An alley cat, plainly – a thieving gitana, he thought, sweatily writhing. Some of the language she'd used when she'd come dragging it in here would have taken the bark off a white oak post. But that wouldn't help. There wasn't nothing going to help if she was bent on putting the dang fool away. No jury this side of the pearly gates was going to run counter to her wants in this matter.

If she just hadn't been so God-awful young!

That, and him keeping her there, could weigh powerful bad in a country that venerated unsullied womanhood.

As she watched his face her lips twisted into a gamin grin. She didn't care what he thought; she could always go higher if he wouldn't cooperate. Lie, bite and gouge – she'd do whatever she had to. It was plain in her eyes, so brazenly scornful. Why did men have to be such damn fools? He grumbled, getting up. "Let's take a look at that critter." She followed him out, complacent as a kitten with a mouthful of feathers.

The "critter" referred to was, according to her story, the means by which she had cut loose of Charlie. A flop-eared dun colored mule with black points – brazen as she was, standing there masticating a jawful of wood pulp cribbed from the tie rail. The sheriff, exasperated, threw out a fist but the spavined monster never backed off a step. He didn't even blink.

Only difference between him and something found at a taxidermist's was the phlegmatic motion of those mangy jaws. The stilt-like locust was so dadburned thin you had to look twice to make sure he was standing there; and McFarron had never set eyes on him before. Not that it mattered. He could still be Charlie's property, tying Medders to this girl tight as matted tail hair.

But of course if no one recognized. . . .

It was the only vestige of hope in sight and the sheriff, reluctantly aware he could procrastinate no longer, untied the critter and with a hard, shuddery breath struck off across the street.

When he hit the end of the lead shank he stopped as though he'd come against a stone wall. The mule, stubbornly set in its tracks, wouldn't budge. Nothing the sheriff tried would move him.

The girl said thoughtfully, "He's probably tired," and McFarron glared, fuming.

"You want somethin' done about this business, or don't you?" he said.

She considered him darkly. "I want Medders brought in. I've got some right," she said grimly.

The sheriff let go of the rope. "So has Medders. Story like that, it's got to be checked. Only concrete fact in sight is this mule. *You* claim it's Charlie's."

"I see. Yes, of course." If that bothered her any it was not apparent. "You want –"

5

"I want him over to Fritchet's livery. If he belongs to Medders somebody will know about it."

She didn't point out all the holes in that notion, just scooped up the rope with a slanchways look, said, "Come Eduardo," and stepped into the sun-scorched dust of the street, the mule lumbering along like a dog at her heels. McFarron, plodding after them, mouthed a bitter curse.

But, breasting the bank, he pulled the chin off his chest. He had his own career to consider and Jones, if there was anything to this yarn, might decide to postpone Charlie's trip to the pen. The sheriff cleared his throat. "We'll step in here."

The girl looked around, eyed the bank and shrugged. She handed Eduardo over to the curb, dropped his rope across the rail and stood coolly waiting on McFarron's pleasure.

He jerked his chin at the doors. "Straight ahead," he grunted, and closed in behind.

A hard faced man in blue serge and brass buttons after scraping them with a raspy glance passed them on into a lobby designed expressly to impress the unwashed hordes that placed their trust in Tiberius Jones.

The girl took in the floor's deep pile, expensive hangings and wrought iron fixtures.

If she was cut down to size she kept it hidden, stood disdainfully waiting for McFarron to make his play.

Beyond the cages and directly in front of the gate to the inner sanctum a blonde sat behind a desk drawn up by the rail. "Good morning, Sheriff," she exclaimed with a smile. "And what can we do for you?"

Imogene Winters, McFarron thought sourly, was as much a part of the bank's facade as the overwhelming rest of the fixtures and furnishings so painstakingly selected to put all comers in a proper frame of mind. She had the charm of Lillian Russell, the face of a Gibson girl and a figure that would turn a man's tongue dry as chalk. She was as efficient as she was breathtaking, and her job was to smile and refuse.

McFarron had been over the route before. "Is the Commissioner in?"

She continued to smile while her gentian eyes, grown increasingly doubtful, assessed the girl with a bright distrust. "He's terribly busy. I'm afraid –"

"You tell him it's about Charlie Medders," the sheriff said, and it was like he'd rubbed Aladdin's lamp. Taking up her pencil the magnificent creature hastily scribbled several words, tore the slip from her pad and passed it to a boy who took it

7

through the rail. In twenty seconds, head bobbing, he was back, and Miss Winters graciously waved them toward the magic portal.

The great man was alone behind an imposing desk whose polished surface was unblemished by even so little as a solitary paper. He did not rise or waste any time on unprofitable amenities. "What about Medders?"

"Might be we've got just about what you want," McFarron announced, indicating the girl. "Belita Storn. Figured you'd want to be the first to hear her story –"

"I've no time for stories."

"That's plain enough." McFarron turned on his heel. "Let's go," he growled, shooing the girl ahead of him.

"Now just a dang minute!" the banker expostulated. "What's a fool girl got to do with that robber?"

"Sometime, mebbe, when you're not so busy –"

"You come back here!" the great man barked, turning purple. "That's an order, Sheriff!"

McFarron, shrugging, reluctantly faced around. Sometimes Jones was powerful hard to take.

"Well . . . ?" the banker rapsed impatiently.

"What's this gypsy got to do with Charlie Medders?"

McFarron rubbed the end of his nose. "Claims she just got away from him. Claims he's been holdin' her incommunicado out to his mine."

"Mine!" Jones cried, like the word made him sick. Looking half strangled he surged from his chair. He was shaking all over. "That salted hole in the ground. . . ." Words seemed to fail him, and the sheriff's sour grin didn't help matters any.

It was the bane of Jones' life that some fairly rich ore Charlie'd passed around last winter had led the great man to make a horrible misjudgment. He had got an assayer's report on the stuff, made sure the claim had been filed and, on the strength of these findings, allowed Medders to borrow fifteen thousand at usurious rates to develop what had shown every evidence of becoming an extremely valuable property.

He had, of course, taken the precaution of drawing up papers for the protection of this loan. But when Medders failed to meet these payments he'd gone out with McFarron to take possession of this gilt-edged collateral. All that could be found was a worked-over dump and an empty hole. Medders had plainly picked up and gone and

9

without leaving even the solace of a forwarding address.

Jones refused to believe it, had been desperately determined they had come to the wrong place. He'd send out a survey gang under Dry Camp Burks, the bank's trouble shooter, but every figure tallied. It was the place, all right. And of course the word got around.

That the wound had not healed was disturbingly evident. "At least," the sheriff said, "he's back in business if you can believe what she says." McFarron tipped a nod at the girl. "Tell him."

She went over it again. She'd set out for Ehrenberg, doing most of her traveling after dark to avoid the heat. The fourth night out they'd been caught up in a sandstorm. They'd been driven off the trail or in any event lost it and that – for this part – was all she could swear to. Medders, and here she was admittedly dependent on the man's version of it, had someway found, rescued, and nursed her back to health.

"How do you know he was Medders?" Jones snapped.

"He told me his name. He'd found me wandering about in the desert, half dead from exposure and thirst. I'd been going around in circles, he said, and the buzzards

10

had led him to me. And barely in time, by his tell of it. All I know is I woke up in this cave, so weak and dizzy I couldn't lift a finger."

She seemed to dig back through a huddle of memories. "Inside it was more like a series of caverns, one leading into another – sometimes two. In the largest of these – it had a queer sort of cabin built into one wall that he always kept padlocked, there was a windlass and some rickety, half rotten ladders that went down into the mine –"

Jones, snorting like a porpoise, waved the rest of it away. That word really irritated him. "You can save your breath," he declared, looking scornful, and reached for his chair as though the interview were over. "I've better things to do than...." Flushing angrily, he snarled: "If that dastard ever dares show his face –"

"If you'd let her tell her story," McFarron said, "it's possible you might find a way to get at him."

The banker stared, testily threw up his hands. "Well . . . all right, but make it short." He looked at his watch. "I'm due at a meeting in about five minutes."

Medders, by her tell, had offered her half the rock they got out in exchange for helping him work it. He would not let her down in

11

the stopes; her job was to bring the ore up with the windlass and pack it in sacks while he was loading again.

Jones said disparagingly: "So, actually, you never *saw* any mine!"

"I saw the ore he sent up." She poked around in her bodice and tossed him a sample.

The banker, catching it, stepped over to the window. McFarron saw his jaw drop, watched the banker get out a penknife and scratch at it and presently thoughtfully stow it in his pocket. Coming back the great man said to Belita, "I presume you know what sort of ore this is?"

She gave him a hard grin. "It's a kind of a keepsake," and put out her hand.

After he'd reluctantly returned the specimen Tiberius Jones very casually suggested it was likely the prettiest piece of the lot.

The girl shook her head. "One of the poorest, really. I swiped this piece because I didn't think he'd miss it or discover I had it on me. Some of those chunks must have been pure silver." She smiled at the greed peering out of Jones' stare. "That vein, in some places, should be a solid foot through and at least a yard wide. It would have to be, judging by what he sent up."

12

"The point," McFarron said, "is what do we do about it?"

II

It was easy to see that Tiberius Jones had clean forgot all about the meeting he had been so anxious to get to. Nor was it hard to imagine the drift of thoughts stimulated by the pictures this girl had set up. But once stung, twice shy, as the old saying went, and cagey suspicions were beginning already to fray the fine edges of the triumph he'd glimpsed. It was just too pat, too good to be true.

The sheriff frowned at him, sighing. "Now what's the matter?"

"Too much hook sticking out of that yarn."

"Hook?" McFarron said, peering around.

"You think it makes sense a hardshell like Medders would let this fluff get out of his sight with a story like that? Smells like sweetening mixed to smear on a trap!" Jones, regarding Belita, snorted. "Five dollars says she's never seen Charlie Medders!"

13

The girl stiffened. Her chin shot out. Her eyes began to snap. Starting toward him she cried, "Whose mule do you reckon is chewing up your hitch rail?"

"Mule? Rail?"

"She claims," the sheriff interpreted, "to have got away from Medders on one of his mules. The monstrosity is tied –"

"Recognize it, do you?"

McFarron grimaced, shaking his head. "But if it does belong to Charlie somebody over at Fritchet's oughta –"

"You don't need to go to all that bother," Belita Storn exclaimed. Eyeing them scornfully, she fished again inside the front of her dress and dug out a paper which she contemptuously tossed on that fine polished desk. Jones stared at the grimy folds as though he looked for a snake to come slithering out. McFarron caught it up. "What's this?" he said, bending to smooth the creases.

"It's the partnership agreement I told you about."

The banker stepped closer, peering over the sheriff's shoulder. In the anxious quiet his sudden intake of breath was disagreeable as a curse. McFarron twisted a look at him. "That Charlie's hand?"

Strangely pale the banker yanked at the

14

bell pull. When the boy put his head in the door Jones growled, "Tell Mr. Turpen I want that Medders folder out of the vault."

As the boy departed the girl sent McFarron a twisted grin and put one hip against an edge of the desk, ignoring the affronted look Jones flung her. She was a cool one all right. The nerve of her won McFarron's grudging respect. She was not one of those he would have cared to play poker with.

Someone knocked at the door; they watched it open. A tall weedy type in black sleeve guards and visor stepped tentatively in with a bulge of folded cardboard. "The Medders account, sir," he said, reaching it out.

Opening it on his desk as far from the girl as the wood allowed, the banker commenced scowlingly to thumb through a sheaf of clipped papers. Picking out a couple he set them down alongside the cause of all this commotion. Covering all but the signature on Belita's paper he signed to his clerk to come take a look. The man bent over, engrossed, at last straightening. "Same hand, I'd say."

Jones beckoned McFarron.

The clerk stepped back. The sheriff, squinting, nodded emphatically. "Looks like you got what you asked for. If Charlie signed those, he signed this one, too. Expect we'll have to accept –"

"I," Jones said, "accept nothing till it's proved."

The sheriff shrugged, not fooled in the least. Anyone could see the banker was hooked. A child could sense the greed working in him.

McFarron picked up his hat. Belita Storn, reaching over, snatched up her agreement. "Here – not so fast," Jones growled, looking testy.

Ignoring him, the girl crammed it into her bodice, the look of her eyes pinning McFarron in his tracks. "Where do you think you're off to now?"

"Might's well get an identification on that mule –"

"What good's that? You already know from his signed agreement –"

"Words," McFarron said, directing a sour smile at Jones. "Marks on a paper don't signify a mine – ain't that so, T.K.?"

The banker, flushing, clenched white fists, looking more than half ready to go up in smoke.

"But he *has!*" the girl cried. "I tell you I *saw* it!"

The sheriff shook his head. "All you saw

16

was the hand picked stuff he sent up for you to look at. How much ore did you see in place? By your own tell, ma'am, you didn't get below that windlass. For all you know that stuff could've been packed in from Tombstone, Tonopah or Ticonderoga."

"It came out of that mine," Belita Storn said doggedly. She whipped the hair back out of her eyes. "Do you think I'm a fool! There was muck on those chunks – the same kind of muck he had on his boots every time he came up!"

McFarron smiled tolerantly. "Have it your way. But if it's that good a deal what'd you want to light out for? You had half comin' just for helpin' him work it. You so wallerin' in wealth you could –"

"I never agreed to be no damn peon!" she yelled, her eyes wild as lightning. "You think I'd stay shut up in that hold with a nut like him? Chained every night like a dog on a wire!" She glared at him, furious. "Lookit my ankles!"

Since she wore no stockings the calloused evidence of shackled was hardly to be denied. The sheriff winced as he looked at the leg she stuck out. It would go hard with Charlie if a jury saw that. Jones, he observed, was trying hard to look shocked, but you could tell by his eyes the kind of thoughts he was hugging.

McFarron asked finally, "Could you dig out the sort of ore she's described fast as ever she could stuff it into sacks? Be reasonable," he grumbled, peering disgustedly at the banker.

But Jones said stubbornly: "You can't talk away those ridges on her legs." Satisfaction glimmered from every cranny of his overfed face. "Just what you'd expect of a scoundrel like Medders – keeping a poor innocent girl penned out there against her will." His jowls shook and joggled like a turkey gobbler's wattles. "Feller ought to be tarred and feathered, by godfreys!"

"Oh, fer cripes sake," McFarron growled, clapping on his hat.

The banker was not distracted. Fatly beaming at the girl he pushed out the overstuffed chair beside his desk, not the visitor's straightback but the one he kept for show. "Miss Storn, you sit right down and be comfortable. You have certainly been through a terrible experience, but now all that's behind – you're not to worry about a thing. We're going to see you get all that's coming to you, believe me. Now ... where'd you say this place is at?"

She'd allowed herself to be ensconced in

18

the overstuffed, spread the tatters of her skirt about those bare and sunbrowned legs. "Why," she said, smiling back at him, "it's out in the desert."

Jones chewed his lip, grinding down on his impatience. "That desert takes in considerable ground."

Belita Storn inclined her head.

He considered her a moment. "I am going to be blunt. Exactly what are you after?"

She didn't boggle over that. "I want him brought in."

"Ah!" Jones nodded with a crafty smile. "You wish your grievances redressed by the court." He looked pleased as Punch. "You want an example made of this feller."

The girl's amber eyes surveyed him. "Not really. I would not care to seem ... vindictive, but...."

"I see," the banker said, rubbing one chubby hand with the palm of the other. "In view of the extreme mental anguish, the confinement and hardships –"

"I'd want only what the court feels is right, Mr. Jones."

The conniving hussy! Butter, McFarron thought, wouldn't have melted in her mouth. Poor Charlie! He felt like shaking her goddam teeth out.

"They're pretty certain to award you

damages," Jones said, and stood a moment, thoughtful. "Only trouble is, with this kind of case there'd have to be a jury, and with juries," he sighed, shaking his head, "you never know. If they're all men, you're in, but it could drag on for months with postponements and adjournments –"

He banged one hand sharply into the other. "You don't have to get tied up in this fashion…there's another, quicker way!"

"There is?" Belita said, eyes opening wide.

The banker nodded. "You could have the money in your hands inside an hour."

"However in the world –"

"Miss Storn," Jones said," "how much is that piece of paper worth to you?"

"My part interest?"

"Up to now," Jones said with a curl of the lip, "all you've got is a scrap of paper. I don't even know that it's binding."

"But you are offering to purchase whatever part in it I've got?"

"My dear young lady. We're just trying to find out what would be best for you. A court case involving a young defenseless female – no matter how it turns out a lot of loose jawed people…Anyway," Jones said, squirming, "if you sold it to me you'd

20

have your money and be out of this thing. Surely –"

"And how much," she asked, "were you thinking to offer?"

"Well..." Jones said, "it's by way of being considerably speculative.... What would you say to five hundred dollars?"

"You really aren't joking?"

"I know," he nodded, "that's a right smart amount of money, but I'd like to feel you've been looked out for...." He broke off to stare, having discovered she was grinning. The more he considered her the less he liked it. His neck got darker and he began to swell up.

Putting aside her amusement she rose to say briskly, "If what you're talking about is an advance...?"

The banker stared. It must belatedly have occurred to him he might have sold her a trifle short, but he was one who could think pretty quick when it came to matters of finance and was able, if he had to, to set up his sights. Patting the sweat and chagrin off his face he tucked his handkerchief away and hiked up his offer to an even five thousand, magnanimously chuckling as he dug out his wallet.

The girl said, glancing around at McFarron, "I guess we've taken up enough of his time. If you're ready now, Sheriff –"

"Here ... hold on!" Jones cried. In a contortion of anguish he came darting forward to catch at her arm. Jaw dropping, he jumped back in ludicrous alarm from the blazing look that banged into his face. "Wh – what's that for?" he spluttered.

"Someone should teach you not to suck eggs." She stood another fierce moment, watching him with a contempt hard to bear. "I suppose that kind of thing is what keeps banks solvent."

Chagrin, the rebellious sting of a man's flustered pride, groped to hold him together above the claws of his fury while he fumblingly attempted to pass it off as a joke. No one joined him in this effort to save face and in the end, McFarron noted, nothing could withstand the livid drive of his cupidity. "Six!" he snarled on the verge of apoplexy.

The girl's knowing eyes were bright with disdain. "And you'd give fifteen thousand for a hole in the ground!" She turned on her heel in a flutter of skirts and sailed through the door without a backward glance.

III

Meanwhile, out in God's open, the man whose actions had set all this in motion was lazily hazing a pair of fat burros through the noontime heat that crawled and writhed above the blistering dust some hundred rods west of the mission San Xavier del Bac, not a great many miles dead south of the crumbling remains of Tucson's old wall.

The gleaming gypsum white of these ancient buildings raised by Indian sweat to the blackrobes' Cross could be seen a good ways across the swales and hogbacks of the Santa Cruz Valley. Charlie Medders, however, had come down off the granite slopes of the saguaro strewn mountains. Lifting the water bag slung from a shoulder he shook it and, grimacing, reluctantly reckoned he better stop by and fill it.

The Jesuits' community had been laid out along the hump of broad sandy knoll somewhat west of the butte whose gaunt whitened cross from time unremembered had stood lonely vigil over the river's gray wastes and the tops of great cottonwoods greenly trembling where they showed above the bluffs. It was the only place in a parched pile of leagues where the north-flowing *Rio de Santa Maria* had managed to maintain a dependable watering place, for mostly it had long since gone underground except during the blessing of infrequent rains. To be sure, at Tucson there was even a lake, but for the bulk of its length the Santa Cruz, as they were calling it now, was so bone dry you couldn't find a frog without you dug halfway to China.

The Sobaipuri Indians – what was left of them – and the Papagos who made this *rancheria* their refuge, someway pieced together a dreary sort of living from the weaving of baskets and a kind of desultory halfhearted farming.

Medders, twisting his head, scanned several fields of drought dwarfed corn beyond the church's far wall as he came up to the coping of the hand-dug well with its skreaky hoist and copper-bound bucket.

He sent the rope down and uncapped his deflated water bag, in a sweat to get through with this and be on his way. Fact is, he would have bypassed the mission as he generally did, except for the needs of his long-eared charges, so hammered-down under the bulge of heavy packs.

24

About to fetch up the bucket, his hand was arrested by the swish of cloth and a rasping crunch of oncoming sandals, and he jerked up his chin with a smothered curse. His worst fears were realized: it was Father Eusebio. The portly padre was making straight for the well.

"Peace be with you, my son."

The benediction was free – like the concerned stretch of smile that tiredly tugged the old man's lips, but the sun bleached stare beneath those tufted brows was reaching for Charlie's fiddle-footed conscience with a zeal the Devil himself could not have broken.

Medders began to back off.

"I think," the priest said, "we'll have an accounting. Where have you been since you last passed this way?"

"Prospectin', Father."

The look in those eyes really made a man squirm.

"Is that what they're calling it now? Salting stripped, worthless holes to sell the unwary?"

Medders looked shocked. "Figured *you*, of all people, would think better o' me than that!" He dragged a sweaty hand across his scraggle of whiskers. Dismay, a weary sadness, limped around through his voice.

25

"The things a man's enemies will tell anymore –"

"Charles," the old man said, cutting into it, "how long has it been since you went to confession?"

Medders loosed a great sigh. "As a matter of plain, unvarnished –"

"The truth, boy."

"Too long," Medders muttered, staring down at cracked boots.

Father Eusebio nodded. "Get yourself cleaned up. I'll be –"

"Golly Moses!" Charlie exclaimed, looking sick. He let go of the well rope. "Ain't a thing I'd rather...." He peered around for his burros. "But I just *can't* stop now! Supposed t' be right this minute in T.K.'s office, an' as a man of my word –"

"The road to hell is paved –"

"You straggly-haired numbskulls! Git outa that cornpatch!" Medders yelled in a passion and, tugging a rock from one of his pockets, let fly with it, furious. "Hup thar!" he shouted. "Git up outa that!" And off he went after them, flapping his arms like a ruptured duck.

Shaking his head, Father Eusebio sighed. Poor Charlie, it looked like, was well on the way to becoming incorrigible. Such a waste of God's talents, the good padre mused.

Something else crossed his mind that was less understandable and, recalling the glitter of the thing Charlie'd thrown, absently fingering his beads he set off to hunt it down.

When he was far enough away to feel beyond the priest's reach, Medders, giving over, hauled up in the shade of an ancient mesquite to mop his steaming brow. That had been a near thing, he told himself, shuddering. A man wanted to be saved, no getting around that, but – like St. Augustine – not right now. Life was too full of a number of things for a gent with red blood to swear off in his prime all the fun and wild pleasures that put the yeast into it.

Then, chancing to glance back, he went rigidly still.

The priest was in the corn moving jerkily about, head down and bent over like a grazing horse, his face scarcely half a foot above the ground. Even as he watched, Charlie saw the padre pounce and come up with something which he vigorously rubbed against a hiked-up fold of his rusty black soutane.

It didn't take Medders hardly a gulp to get the connection between that rock he'd pitched at Begat and Begetta and the something the old man was so engrossedly studying.

In his sudden perturbation Medders felt half minded to go reclaim the chunk of ore. It was one of his carefully culled jewelry specimens, of about the same weight and worth as the little gleaming beauty that skirted jezebel had made off with after all them fine words about soul mates and marriage and the wonderful tomorrows they could share in double harness. Women!

Charlie snorted.

Worse than the seven years' itch. Back a man into a corner and take the dang fillin's right out of his teeth! He had learned about women before he'd turned twenty – enough to know better than swaller the hogwash this Belita Storn filly had been painting the cave with whilst running sly fingers through his rumpled hair!

She was an armful, all right – cuddly as a kitten. But Charlie Medders, though he might not look it, had been around a fortnight and wasn't to be caught up in no kind of net like that. Cheaper to give her a full half interest and stake that Eduardo mule out where she could get hold of him. Worth half the mine to be rid of her, he'd thought. And, proving him right, off she'd gone like a shot.

28

Well, she'd talk, like enough. Probably yak her fool head off, so it didn't too much matter about that chunk the padre was fisting. Might even tend to confuse things a little. Might even turn out that a few more wouldn't be wasted if left to be found where these school boys could peddle them.

Tramping after his burros, sweating and mumbling, he put out the bait until his pockets were empty, setting up the last bit in the center of the trail where it made the big loop snaking down to the crossing.

Didn't make no never-mind to Charlie who came onto it. As redskins went these was educated hombres. Any Papago would savvy a hunk of rock rich as this could be wink quick swapped for a snootful of firewater. So let 'em, and to hell with it! Give T.K. something to think about, maybe.

Despite that whopper he had told the priest nothing could have been more remote from his intentions than to find himself closeted with T.K. Jones. When he'd set off on this pack trip three days ago Phoenix had been his avowed destination. But, following Eduardo's tracks, more enticing notions had intervened.

What, after all, could that overstuffed hog of a banker do? A man got bored with hiding out; and it wasn't like Medders had done anything a gent could really be jugged for. If Jones hadn't been so stinking anxious to buy, heckling and pestering to get in on what his own grasping mind had built into a bonanza, he would never have got bit. It was T.K.'s own perseverance that had fashioned the coup, suggesting the soft touch by which Charlie Medders had latched onto a cool fifteen thousand with nothing but a gutted hole for collateral.

Of course Jones had squawked. It had impaired his public image, made him look a bloody fool. So what? With his plasters and liens and wholesale foreclosures he had weaseled into everything of worth inside a hundred and fifty miles, and had no more compunctions than could be found in a vulture. Hell, he'd been *asking* for it! And everybody knew it.

Now if a feller could put any dependence in a female...but such preposterous thoughts was plumb ridiculous. Medders knew from a heap of sad remembrances you couldn't. Why, that dangfool critter might end up in Hermosillo! Sure, he'd slipped into their conversations every landmark she'd need to see her safely into Tucson, but it was no guarantee she had got there. Second day out a wind had sprung up; he never had come onto that mule's tracks again. She could have wound up in Globe, or Winkelman, or Ajo.

Her guile and excitements might have led some fellers right up the garden path. She had played it pretty slick, making out to be lost and half out of her head – he'd thought for a while she really was. And then, convalescing, all them blandishments and calf's eyes. It wasn't that Medders had been less susceptible that had led him to see through her artful dodges; he'd been long enough around to have had most of these enticements worked on him before. So he'd put out bait, offered her half the lode in exchange for a little fabricated help, and to prove that he meant business had put it down in writing.

She'd eased up some then, not dropping him like no hot potato but not pushing any more on the rose-colored wonders of life in double harness. Then he'd staked out the mule, and off she'd gone.

When he had tucked those mileposts into the evening gab fests he had not, of course, been figuring to pull Jones into this, only trying to make sure that in ridding himself of her she didn't come to grief. But the more he'd got to mulling it over the better the whole thing looked with Jones cast again in the role of big fish. It could be a real lark!

Putting one over on Tiberius Jones had been the kind of thing a man could date time by, and if it happened again the lard-bottomed skinflint might be laughed clean out of the golrammed country. A lot of those who in the past had been so free with their jeers could be glad to shake the hand of a man who accomplished that. Might even be hailed as a public benefactor!

Caught up in so salubrious a prospect it seemed no time at all until Medders found himself and burros churning up the dust of Tucson's *barrio libre,* the old part of town that led past Sol Warner's store off the Plaza de Armas, a saddle maker's shop, assayer's office and three-four saloons before in a jogging hit-or-miss fashion the way opened up to disclose the turreted structure housing T.K.'s abominated bank.

One might suppose he would have used a little more caution in the manner of his approach, but it never occurred to Charlie's day-dreaming mind the girl might have gone to the sheriff about those scars, thinking to grab it all, or that she knew more about this ore he'd found than he did.

IV

First stop, he reckoned, might as well be Tiny O'Toole's. He wanted to get this ore off his hands before T.K. got out an order restraining him and, while the town had more firms engaged in assaying than the amount of moved ore appeared honestly to warrant, none of the others had O'Toole's unique facilities. With the ore disposed of he could leave Begat and Begetta with Frichet while he sought and enjoyed the ministrations of a barber, got himself some new duds and helped the word get round that Charlie Medders, dang his eyes, had finally made a real winning.

Physically O'Toole was a strapping big six-footer with a black Irish mug, hands like hams, and a mind that was sharper than the proverbial steel trap. Sizing up the burros' packs from behind his stone filled windows, he came out on the street in his stained leather apron to wring Medders' fist like a jovial bear.

"Let's git this stuff under cover," Charlie grumbled, cutting short the offered pleasantries with a nervous scowl. "This'll have to be fer cash an' I ain't figurin' to do much standing around."

O'Toole, saying nothing, merely jerked his chin.

Charlie threw off the ropes and the big Irishman helped manhandle the packs while the burros, snuffling, began to hunt round for a good place to roll.

Inside, with the first of the sacks opened up and the contents spilled across the top of a counter, Medders stood fidgeting in a squirm of impatience while the misnamed mick considered the ore, once or twice picking up a piece to thoughtfully handle, even lifting one chunk into the garish arc of an over-head Rochester. When, finally, he turned to reach for a hammer, Medders said testily: "Never mind that! Just make me a price!"

O'Toole hung a hip on the counter and stared. He knocked out a brier, scooped it full, tamped and lighted it, still with the blue of his look darkly digging. Through swirls of layering smoke he said thinly, "Twenty-eight hundred."

Medders, livid, commenced stuffing the ore back into his sack.

"Four thousand." O'Toole sighed.

34

Charlie said, glaring: "This ain't stolen ore –"

"Then why such a tearin' sweat to be shed of it?"

"Because," Medders growled, "I don't want it impounded," and O'Toole showed his teeth.

"Now ye're talkin'. Takes some doin' to get ahead of Jones. His bank got out a restrainin' order right after you took to the brush. Every assayer in town's been warned. Where you think that leaves *me* if he decides to come down on it?"

"But he can't!" Medders snarled.

O'Toole asked, scornful, "Which of the hierarchy did you git that from? You ever hear of a time inside this county when T.K. Jones, the almight Tiberius, could not seize an' gobble anything he put his mind to?"

"But . . . Hell," Charlie protested, "once it's outa my hands –"

"You don't know that." The blue-jowled Irishman peered irascibly. "I'll go to fifty-two hundred."

"Jesus H. Christ!" Charlie pawed at his face. "The four of them sacks'll run close t' ten thousand!"

"Well," O'Toole grimaced, dusting off his dukes, "I got to have some kind of margin. Besides, it's peculiar."

35

"If you mean that muck –"

"I'm talkin' about the color."

Charlie's eyes rolled. "It's practically *pure silver!*"

"You heard me. Fifty-two hundred, an' that's as far as I'll go. If it's in your head some nump will cough up more you better go grab it. But don't," he warned darkly, "come wailin' at me if McFarron tromps in afore ye've pocketed yer money."

Medders swore in a passion, but he knew O'Toole had him. Nobody else with enough ready cash was like to risk crossing up the county's biggest mogul just to stay on trading terms with a bum like Charlie Medders. If he did dig up so wild a gambler there was no guarantee he'd come out any better.

And the longer he took setting up a deal the greater the peril of the sheriff stepping in on the strength of that paper Jones had got from the court.

It went sore against his grain to give in but he could see, still fuming, it was either give in or chance having the whole dratted haul took away from him. And he would almost sooner *give* it away than see it scooped up by that straggly-haired banker!

"You win," he grumbled. But it just wasn't in him to take a licking with good grace. Stomping around like a sore-footed

36

bull while the Irishman was getting the hard cash from his safe, Charlie went on at some length and then started all over. "What really gets me goin'," he growled, "is to think all this time I been considerin' you a *friend!*"

This seemed a pretty harsh indictment but O'Toole went coolly on with his counting. Stacking up the last bulging handful of twenties the Irishman shut his safe, spun the dial and, arms akimbo, considered Medders sourly.

"Fifty-two hundred, coin of the realm. Now suppose you take it an' git the hell out av here."

"Why, you liver eatin' hound!" Charlie cried, affronted, and stepped back to give himself room to square off. "I'm goin' to –"

"So it's a fight ye're wantin' now then, is it?" O'Toole, nothing loath, began to roll up his sleeves. He was just moving forward when a man tore in off the street, pop eyed and panting. "The sheriff!" he gasped, and seemed to have used all the breath he had left.

Medders spun toward the window, cursed, and white-cheeked lunged for the mound of gleaming coins. As he crammed them frantically into his pockets it became all too apparent he would run out of space before he ran out of dollars.

37

O'Toole, watching, grinned. If he had any worries about his own part in this, such qualms did not noticeably impair his amusement.

"Fer cripes sake," Medders howled, copiously perspiring, "hurry up, you guys, an' give me a hand!"

Nobody moved.

The bloke who'd run in off the street with the news stood goggling – still heaving and puffing – like Charlie was some kind of two-headed freak. And O'Toole, in his enjoyment, was a hard cross to bear. "Reminds me," he said, "of the half starved mouse that got into the corncrib and stuffed so hearty he couldn't git out."

Medders, looking around wildly, began turning out his pockets, disgorging silver dollars in a desperate attempt to make room for those stacks of gleaming gold eagles – but there just wasn't time. With a last despairing snarl – too hurried even to unload his spleen in the ominous crunch of that approaching tread – Charlie scooped all he could into his up-ended hat and made a staggering bolt for the shop's rear door.

V

The Irishman, wiping his eyes, looked to be in the final shakes of a belly laugh when Tiberius Jones slammed into the place with a red headed woman practically riding his heels. She had the hard used appearance of a fortune teller put through the brush by a pack of disgruntled housewives.

Blinking, O'Toole, in a kind of double take, astonishedly returned the girl's appraising stare. Besides being almost painfully young she was, he discovered, in some outlandish gypsyish fashion extraordinarily attractive. Thus engaged, he did not at once realize McFarron had not stepped in with them. When this caught at his notice he put the girl out of mind and considered Jones warily.

The banker's protuberant eyes, prowling the shop, wheeled like a pair of hovering vultures to disquietingly fasten O'Toole in his tracks. "You find my presence humorous?" he asked, staring nastily; then said, harsh as Moses about to seize the golden calf: *"Where is he?"*

O'Toole looked puzzled, but Jones was not in any game-playing mood. Impatient, testy, the lash of his glance snaking past the big Irishman's blocking shape spied the glint of spilled coins and stopped, bright as fire, against the ore cluttered counter.

His lips spread thin in a yellow grin. "Where'd *that* come from?"

O'Toole said, surprised, "Them sacks, you mean?" and wheeled back, disgusted. "More of that loco desert rat junk –"

"Don't look like junk to me," Jones growled, brushing past the assayer for a closer stare. Snatching up a piece, cheeks flushed and furious, he thrust it under O'Toole's twitching nose. "You call that 'junk'? It's damn near solid silver!"

The Irishman, snorting, peered at the banker like he thought T.K. had gone off his rocker. "That greenish lookin' crap?" He loosed a dubious cackle. "Pullin' my leg, eh? Look – I'm laughin'."

Jones wasn't laughing. "You ran a test on this stuff?"

"A test, the man says!" O'Toole rolled his eyes. "Chri'sake, T.K., silver's black – it ain't *green!*"

"Sure, sure. You run some of this through the works right away. I'll foot the bill," the banker smiled, standing back.

40

O'Toole chewed his cheek. "I can't do that."

"Then what would you say if I impounded this ore and had the court –"

"I don't think you could get away with it," O'Toole said, sweating. "Public opinion –"

"The public," Jones said, "are a bunch of damn sheep, and you know it!"

O'Toole had too much tied up in this to throw in his hand if he could find a way around it. With a show of confidence he said, crisply blunt: "That court order you got hardly gives you a license to grab everything you happen to fancy."

A tide of red crept above the banker's tight fitting collar; his eyes bulged more noticeably. Then a scornful smile nastily twisted his mouth. "I imagine the Court in its continued good judgment, once the facts are exposed, will decide in the bank's favor." He threw up an imperious hand as the Irishman's impatience seemed about to interrupt. "The restraint, it is true, was imposed against Medders, but if you're bursting to point out this ore does not belong to him I would advise you to consider the following circumstances.

"First of all," Jones smiled, "this un-principled swindler – and I'm speaking of Medders – was observed to enter town with

41

two heavily laden burros known, I believe, as Begat and Begetta. Those animals, stripped of their packs, are presently standing outside this shop. You have a table that is covered with a lot of high-grade specimens and three unopened packs."

He paused to stab a triumphant glance across the shine of dropped coins. "And I would remind you," he said, his satisfaction crammed with malice, "that all assayers, including yourself, were apprised of the Court's order and warned against buying any ore from Charlie Medders. Now," he chuckled, insufferably pleasant, as Andy McFarron sauntered in from out back, "if you want to claim this ore, put yourself on record."

"You all through?" O'Toole asked.

"Just answer the question. Is this your ore or isn't it?"

"I don't quite see –"

"All we want out of you is an answer!"

"I think," said the sheriff as O'Toole's jaw tightened, "you won't do yourself any good bein' stubborn."

A shine of sweat slicked the Irishman's cheeks and his glance clawed around like a wet footed cat while McFarron stood watching for a sign from the banker and the deepening silence grew increasingly uncomfortable.

When he could stand it no longer O'Toole pulled up his head and on a bitter outrush of breath declared the ore didn't belong to Medders.

Jones and the sheriff exchanged unreadable looks. "Then it's yours?" the banker prompted.

"I haven't said so."

"Maybe you won't have to."

"I expect," McFarron drawled, "you know how it happens to be settin' on that bench."

"A desert rat –"

"Sure," Jones grinned. "A rat named Charlie Medders."

When the assayer failed to respond the banker said to McFarron: "Bring in your prisoner, Sheriff."

McFarron said gruffly, "I don't have a prisoner. Wasn't nobody out there."

O'Toole, finding hope, showed a dry lift of lips.

"Well, no matter," Jones said, darkly eyeing his sheriff. "I believe we can show to the court's satisfaction it was Medders, all right, that fetched the stuff in here." He slanched a glance at the girl. "Show Mr. O'Toole that specimen you fetched from Medders' mine, my dear."

The girl stared back, looking fussed and balky, but finally dug the little chunk from her bodice and dropped it into the banker's outstretched palm. Jones, beckoning the assayer, went back to the bench and placed the sample beside one of the bigger hunks. "What do you think the Court will say to that?"

There was no room for argument. The greenish tinge was evident throughout. Both pieces had obviously come from the same source.

O'Toole fidgeted. "Hell, I don't know where she got it!" he blustered. But his eyes looked sick.

The banker laughed. "She got it from Medders' cave, as we'll prove." He picked up the girl's sample and stood a while, grinning. "you want to change your story while you still got time?"

O'Toole's eyes looked mean, the whole shape of him sullen with the kind of frustration a man could hardly bear. He finally said stubbornly, "All you've got to hook this ore up to Medders is a lot of fool talk!"

"We've got more than that." Jones peered at him smugly. "This girl is Medders'

44

partner with a full half interest in every ounce he sells – what's more, she's got it sewed up in writing, and chain marks on her legs to prove the chiseling son of a bitch has been keeping her penned up out there like a goddam peon! McFarron," he said, "you've got the court's warrant. I want this ore, every piece of it, impounded."

O'Toole, gnashing his teeth, waved his arms like crazy. "God damn it," he cried, "you can't –"

"Before I get through I'll have you *both* behind bars," the banker said with the tone and look one might expect of a man so vindictively self-righteous. He was like a cat having fun with a mouse. "Most silver," he said, "as you yourself pointed out, in its natural state generally tends to seem dark, sometimes almost black as it comes from the ground – which is not to say it can never look green. One source," he declared with considerable satisfaction, "discovered in this vicinity during the Spanish occupation, had this strange peculiarity. It came from the Weeping Widow, one of the fabulous Lost Padre mines."

If the implication had not been so outrageous, if O'Toole had not been so bitterly preoccupied with his own frustrations and probable plight, he might have

45

noticed the pallor, the rigid stance of the girl.

Neither man did, but O'Toole cried, incredulous: "You figure Medders has stumbled onto it?"

"That will be our contention when we take this to court."

VI

At about the point where the sheriff got to wondering if Charlie Medders had any idea what sort of prospect he was fiddling around with, the subject of this not uncharitable speculation was inspecting his reflected splendour in the full-length glass of The Boston Store – R.G. Appopolus, Prop.

Bathed, barbered and freshly outfitted from forty dollar benchmade boots to the finest product of the John B. Stetson (cowman's hat) Company, it might be reasonably assumed the gentleman in question was basking not only in the best of health but enjoying the good fortune of a carefree mind.

As a matter of fact, he looked rather glum. Despite being taken advantage of and suckered into leaving more behind than he could stomach, he was again in funds, had outsmarted T.K. and should have been sitting on top of the world. It was what he'd been telling himself ever since, stumbling out of O'Toole's back door, he'd run smack into the arms of Sheriff Andy McFarron.

To be sure, the dour Scot had preached a pretty stern sermon before stepping aside to let him pass, but this sort of thing – coming in at one ear and leaving by the other – could hardly be charged with upsetting a man. Of course Andy had turned him loose – what *else* could he have done? Hadn't the pair of them been compadres all the way back to Slaughter? Cripes, wasn't that what a man's friends was for?

Only thing McFarron had told him he hadn't already known, or suspected, was that cussed girl running to the law with her unvarnished whoppers and – more disgusting – teaming up with Jones to whipsaw him out of this caveful of silver.

Well, hell, he reflected, what could you expect of a thieving gitana, and a female at that! It was the dang ungratefulness of it that gnawed him – selling half the share he had plain outright *give* her, and to of all people that straggly haired banker!

Though enough to make a polecat cuss this
47

was not, strictly speaking, the rock-bottomed source of Medders' fluttery disquiet. Leastways he did not think it was, but he had a nagging jumpety hunch he wasn't going to feel better till he got out of this burg.

Which was what Sheriff Andy had advised him to do. But a gent that was free, white and old enough to vote was bound to do some toe-dragging before letting any ham-hocked, hog-faced, weasel-eyed grabber of widders' mites and old ladies' homesteads put him on public notice. Folks might reckon the durn cottonmouth had sure enough sent him packing! Danged if he'd give them that much satisfaction.

Confidence thus precariously bolstered, fed up with all those precautionary antics which had so far kept him out of Jones' clutches, Charlie forthwith quit his safe obscurity to sally forth into the lamplit shadows of the town's main drag. This was still a free country. Jones' bank might control its purse strings but the streets belonged to nobody. Not even Belita Storn with her lies could have him picked up without due process.

It was this which had finally decided him. His new wealth was hot as live coals in his pockets, and a gent which had spent six

48

months in the brush craved something more exciting than bare walls to look at.

About to step into the Red Herring for a beer, a bleary eyed galoot floundering out of the place blundered roughly into him. With the stench of a bar rag the fellow pushed free then began, like a bullwhacker, to dress Medders down.

It was Phineas O'Toole, the barrel-chested assayer who had got Charlie's high-grade for half its worth, guffawing like a loony when Medders had been stampeded into leaving part of that.

He wasn't laughing now. The bleary eyes, regarding Charlie's fine clothes, suddenly flared with a savage recognition. Drunk and unmistakably ugly he thrust his glowering face into Charlie's, grabbed a fistful of shirtfront and, wheeling, slammed Medders furiously against a wall. "Ye pussy-footin' crook! I've a moind," he snarled, "t' take it out av yer hide!"

Medders, too breathless and shaken for speech, had enough red fox curling round through his makeup to know the better part of valor held no brief for broken bones. Going limp and loose in every joint he hung from the assayer's brawny grip looking pitiful and wilted as a yanked-up flower.

Startled, O'Toole peered down at him.

Snarling with disgust he pitched the sagging weight aside to stare drop-jawed and ludicrous as Medders, bounding to his feet, struck off into the coagulating shadows with no more ado than a departing mosquito.

With a shout of rage the big Irishman took after him.

Medders, hearing the plunging strike of those boots banging nearer and louder at every heart jolting stride, didn't need any diagrams to guess what would happen if those whopping great fists laid hold of him again. McFarron, he reckoned, must have grabbed all that ore. O'Toole, at the very least, would clean Charlie's pockets. In his present state of mind the man might cripple him for life!

A dozen brash expedients clawed through the churn of Charlie's thoughts, but there was little time for cleverness and none at all for dodges. If the assayer latched onto him about the best a man could hope for was that some passer-by might stop to sweep up the pieces. Medders didn't dare swap words with O'Toole and it began to sink in he wasn't about to outrun him.

The man's lunging breath wa shot against his neck – he could picture those hair-matted arms reaching for him. There was one crazy chance and, desperately, Charlie took it.

Gasping and wheezing he dug in his heels and went down in a convulsive twisting fall. He heard the Irishman curse, but the man couldn't catch himself. Something crashed agonizingly against Charlie's hip as O'Toole, banging into him, went ass over elbows to land spraddled out in a teeth-cracking sprawl.

Charlie wasted no time trying to help the guy up. Hardly pausing to feel himself over he took off and got out by the shortest route.

But Phineas O'Toole was not a man easily shaken.

Medders knew before he'd gone half a block the fellow was after him. He tried to lose the assayer in a maze of dark alleys. Glancing back as he came forth with ragged breath into the lamp-laced traffic of Meyer Street, Charlie cursed. The guy was a regular bloodhound!

Shoving frantically across a pedestrian crammed walk Medders dashed recklessly into the street, wildly diving in front of a twelve-horse hitch. Skirting a hack, barely missed by the wheels, scarcely hearing the angry yells of its driver, he ducked through a rack of tied pones and, in sheer desperation, flung himself through the batwings of Tony Florido's swank Carleton House bar.

51

It was the only safe place he could think
of. A kind of sanctum sanctorum, the retreat
of big business, it had become over the years
a sort of unofficial club for the town's top
strata citizens, gents like Sol Warner, Digby
Rhodes, Hiram Walker, Archie Bell and
other big moguls of the mining, cattle and
mercantile trades. No bums were allowed,
no brawls tolerated; and Charlie Medders,
who had never passed through its varnished
portal before. looked around in awe at the
plush upholstering, panelled woodwork, the
whole overwhelming aroma of elegance.

With a sigh of relief Medders headed for
the bar, pleased to discover that, except for
hired help and several well dressed gents
with their silk tiled heads bent over a far
table, the place at this early hour was
practically deserted.

Just as he was fixing to plop a hoof on the
rail the baldheaded barkeep, leaning forward
confidentially, said *sotto voce* above the glass
he had been polishing: "Ain't you got into
the wrong pew, Jack?"

Suspiciously sniffing Medders peered at
him, puzzled; and just about there someone
dug his sore ribs with a mighty rude elbow.
"Outside, Mac, an' don't give me no sass."

Charlie, twisting his head, beheld a burly
shape in tails and stiff shirt grimly flexing its

muscles perhaps a half a step away. With that off-center nose, battered ears and outthrust jaw the guy was obviously a bouncer.

Instinctively backing off a bit, uncomfortably aware of the road grime and the gaping torn knee of one split trouser leg, Medders had a disquieting vision of O'Toole hunched and waiting just beyond the varnished doors.

The skin began to darken in irate patches about his ears. Swelling up, he said affronted, "You're talkin' to a man which could buy this dump an' tear it down!" He slapped a handful of double eagles ringing on the bar. "Set 'em up," he said, "the drinks are on –"

The bouncer dropped a splayed paw on his arm. From the corner of a steel-trap mouth he rasped: "Out!" with a jerk of the jaw in the direction of the street.

Medders shook off the hand. Peering arrogantly down the length of his nose he tapped the man's chest. "Do you know who I am?"

The man, big enough almost to make two of Medders, seemed taken aback and Charlie, thus encouraged, swung around to the barkeep. "Come, come, my good man," he cried, pounding a rock-scarred fist on the bar. "The drinks are on me, and there's the cash to –"

"Takes more than cash," the baldheaded stated, "to stand treat in this place. First you've got to belong. An' you're six hundred short," he sighed, dribbling the gold like checks through stacked fingers, "of havin' the price."

"What?" Medders goggled. "One thousand dollars!" He stared, aghast.

"It's a gentleman's club."

Charlie pulled himself together. "Well, all right," he muttered, and counted another six hundred onto the bar. "There! I guess that does it. Now set 'em up fer –"

"Man," the barkeep sighed, "don't you hear good? I told you this here is a *gentleman's* club."

Charlie said, snorting, "It would have to be at that price! Well, what're you waitin' on? You've got my money –"

"It ain't a question of money. You gotta be asked," the baldhead grinned, and gave his bouncer the nod.

Charlie never had a chance. A fist exploded against his head. He spun backwards, sagging, bringing up against the bar. Something slugged him in the stomach with the whack of a mule's hind hoof and the floor rushed up, dissolving like a burst egg.

He felt himself being lifted. He got back enough vision to see the boards blur beneath

54

him, to have a peculiar sense of flying. Then his head cracked the batwings and he went through, still scrabbling with ineffectual hands, to sail hurtling across the rough planks of the walk toward a wild lifting tangle of steel-shod hoofs.

The spooked broncs tore away, dragging the snapped-off rail.

When he collected enough gumption to think of picking himself up, the first thing Charlie's groggy stare fastened onto was the toothy grin of Tiberius Jones.

VII

Too stunned to cuss, too bushed to run, Medders stood like Chicken Little waiting for the sky to fall, eyes bugged out like knots on a stick. Jones, exuding satisfaction, looked tickled as Delilah peering down at shorn Samson or Salome viewing the head of dead John.

As the first awful grip of his fright began to loosen, Charlie's stare, quickened by hope, anxiously prowled the hemming faces, finding little to reassure him.

Long ago he'd exhausted the last vestige

of his credit, sacrificing friendship to a miscellany of pranks, repaying people's patience with a clatter of unkept promises. Now, with a caveful of silver, needing only time to move it, he was flanked by the claws of this grinning Legree and no one, it looked like, would say a stinking word for him.

He burned to tell them what he had – that he could pay every claim, and with a heaped high bonus for those who had waited longest, but it would be wasted breath. He was the unhappy veteran of too many strikes which had failed to pan out. They were glad to see him caught up with.

It was the measure of their remembering contempt that, while they had no love for Tiberius Jones, not one of these hardshells would lift a finger to shield Charlie Medders from this polecat's revenge.

No, not one.

Hauling his chin up he twisted a look about.

"Why, Charles," Jones said, "is that truly you?"

Ignoring the titters, Medders brushed himself off. "I've been throwed out of better places," he growled, counting faces. But he could not find McFarron's and interpreted this to be an ominous sign.

Being jailed was not the worst that could

happen. Jones had his big casino with him – Dry Camp Burks, that would no more worry about potting a guy than he would at discovering a worm in his chawing.

Charlie felt his scraped jaw. Didn't no one need to spell out his plight; he was between a rock and a hard place for sure, and if he got loose of this he was not going to be caught again – no matter how it looked – without some kind of a handle he could grab for. Leaving his gun in his room had been a pretty dumb stunt, but he was danged if he would beg!

Jones with a widening grin observed, "Appears you've about reached the end of your tether." When this got no answer he said, nastily chuckling, "I guess you're all squared off to pay back that loan."

It got powerfully quiet, all those counter-jumpers holding their breaths, so glued to their listening they couldn't even swallow. Yet what could he say? What *dared* he say?

A gent was perfectly willing to take care of his obligations, but how could you know after all this while which were real and which drummed up to take advantage of his predicament?

The more he peered the madder Charlie got. Nobody wants to be backed into a corner; and if he paid out one dime the whole push would be after him. Why, half of them slobs was droolin' right now!

He covered his fears with a scowl and stood pat; whereupon, with some unction, the great man suggested they adjourn someplace and have a shareholders' meeting.

"Shareholders!"

Medders came out of his shell with a shout. With a fist shaken furiously under Jones' nose he cried: "You ain't goin' to move in on *me* like that! You think I was born yesterday?"

The banker said with curled lip: "You came into this town with four sacks of ore which the sheriff, by court order, has impounded. In your packratting around you've obviously stumbled onto something." He looked about to say more, but changed his mind when his glance, rather irritably, took note of the gaping faces. He said, motioning curtly, "I think we had better step over to my office."

Medders wanted no part of any bind like that. "You got anythin' to say you can say it right here – in front of witnesses, by grab." He held up his ripped trouser leg. "I ain't trustin' myself alone again with your plug-uglies!"

The implication, though little better than a barefaced lie, served to turn Jones cautious.

58

Enough so that when the hard-faced Burks started toward Medders, glancing back for the high sign, the banker reluctantly shook his head. The rough stuff would keep.

Few knew better than Tiberius Jones how unstably fickle a crowd's whim could be, and right now these galoots, themselves whipsawed by this slickery customer, stood squarely behind him. He did not often have so comforting a feeling.

His intentions toward Medders had not changed in the least but there were other ways than violence of getting at the man. Appearing nettled he said: "I am not here to argue. What these gentlemen want is some sort of installment against the bills you've run up. A little earnest money," he suggested, smiling when the shopkeepers growled. "Is that too much to ask?"

"Well...no." Charlie, feeling through his clothes, was not as stupid as he looked. He could bend with the wind if that were the lesser of two hateful courses. "I'd admire to do what's right. You divvy this up the way you reckon is best. Hold out your hat," he grumbled, and emptied his pockets.

The alacrity of his capitulation darkly sharpened the banker's stare but, concealing his annoyance, Jones toted up the coins and currency, saying at last in deeper disgruntlement, "I make it four hundred, seventy-eight dollars and forty-seven cents."

The merchants, looking thunderstruck, regarded the banker with considerable suspicion. Jones colored angrily. "Where's the rest of it? You got more than that!"

Charlie sighing, slung wide both arms. "Well, look for yerself – don't take my word for it."

Jones glared, speechless; and Burks, shifting his chew, said, "I'll git it out of him!"

"Here – wait," Jones cried, and Burks spat disgustedly. But the banker couldn't afford to make a martyr of Charlie; not, anyway, at this stage of the game. "All you boys that have a claim against Medders, if you'll step round to the bank tomorrow with your figures, can have a pro rata share of what he's turned over. Meanwhile –"

"That's right," Charlie grinned, "show up an' git yer dimes an' nickels, because you can bet yer bottom dollar that's all there'll be when his bank gits done with it."

Jones winced, but he had seen this coming and hung onto his temper. "Meanwhile," he said, speaking up strong to put the heat back on Medders, "we'll have a stockholder's meeting at one o'clock sharp and issue shares in this strike –"

60

"Oh, no you don't!"

Charlie, carried away by the enormity of this proposal, flashed his teeth like a cornered wolf. "You're not slicin' up any find of mine to put yourself in good with these counter-jumpers! You may own the bank an' two-thirds of this town but you ain't puttin' me through that kinda hoop! What's mine is mine an' –"

"You see the kind of crook we're up against," Jones said. "But I assure you, gentlemen, the law will prevail. You shall have your just shares –"

"There *ain't* no shares!" Charlie yelled, beside himself. "All's I've got . . ."

"We know what you've got," the banker spoke to the crowd, "and you can't turn your back, now you've struck it rich, on all these fellows who have clothed you and fed you and kept you going the Lord only knows how many weary months when except for them you would have starved to death." He considered Charlie with considerable dis-taste, suddenly disclaiming in a loud and terrible voice, "Do you deny that these good people have kept you afloat?"

Medders found himself boxed. He tried to get off the hook with the disparaging concession that, "If you want to call a few sacks of rusty beans, some castoff jeans an'

61

a old coat or two −" but the growls this brought on made him falter and stop.

He began to sweat and his skin felt full of prickles. "All right," he snarled, putting the best face he could on it, "I'm no ingrate! Some of these gents has sure-enough helped me an' I'll take care of 'em − but that don't mean I'll let a whoppyjawed loan shark carve up my winnin' like I hadn't no rights! Who the hell found it, that's what *I* wanta know! Not *him!*" Medders shouted, with a look no real man could possibly abide.

But the only looks which mattered to Jones was how this looked − or might be made to look − to these yokels who made up the consensus of public opinion.

With these in mind he said, tired but patient, "All we require is that you satisfy your debts. To those who've helped little some small token should be given, each in just measure, while those who have borne the brunt of your finagling should be recompensed, obviously, in like proportion. Now, wait −" he cautioned, holding up a hand as Medders appeared about to jump from his pants. "You can treat everyone fairly and still have the lion's share left for yourself. You've only to form a company, float some stock −"

"An' find myself with the widders an'

orphans! I ain't fallin' fer that," Charlie said with a sneer.

Jones considered him. "I rather imagine you will." Then he said sharp and clear: "Or do you want to be hailed into court to face that girl?"

"Girl!" Medders cried, staring about wildly. "*What* girl?"

"Is there more than one?" The banker said caustically, "I'm surprised you haven't been tarred and feathered."

Though Charlie waved clenched fists and, snarling, denied in opprobrious language even the faintest idea of what Jones was driving at, it was evident to all that this was nothing but bluster. The mean look of his eyes, the blotched cheeks, told the story.

"The choice," Jones said, "is yours; but if I have to I'll put Belita Storn on the stand and let her tell what happened to her out in those hills and down..."

But Medders, cursing, had already fled.

VIII

With his burros Medders spent the shank of that night in the mountains high above the robbers' roost men called Tucson, scowling at the jumble of flittery lights glowing like jewels from the ghostly dark that hid dusty streets and trash littered alleys. He'd been too upset to go back to his room for what was left of the money he had got from O'Toole. So filled with alarm at what the banker had said and by things implied, he had even come away without the supplies he'd gone in for.

He was still in a muddle of confused apprehensions as he watched gray dawn begin to creep up out of the east. Who could guess what kind of rotten deal a skunk slick as Jones might have talked that girl into! Or what lies she had told in the grip of ambitions put into her head by the banker's glib whoppers! According to McFarron she had already been tricked into handing Jones half of the half interest Charlie, in a kind of moon madness, had so impulsively given her.

He was caught in the tug of conflicting desires.

64

Every instinct honed by danger urged toward flight while the way was still open. Other notions, equally fierce and quite as bitterly compelling, made Medders reluctant to take to the brush while the banker – justified by frustrated creditors – proceeded to cut up Charlie's find and take over.

The bastard could get away with it, too! No one had to tell Charlie. With that girl on his side and the law in his pocket Jones could ride roughshod over Medders' objections, do just about anything he wanted with the property. Who was to stop him? He could marshal control of fifty percent. he could do just what he had said he would – form a company, float stock and, in Charlie's absence, juggle things around to suit himself. He could buy up the notes Charlie'd given those merchants, then sue for a judgment and use Charlie's shares to pay himself off with. There was no damned end to the things he might do.

When it came to skullduggery you had to stay up all night if you hoped to stay even with T.K. Jones!

Medders cursed in a passion and shook both fists.

This was why he'd pulled out of his run to wait here where he could see if the banker meant to have him followed. He couldn't believe Jones would pass up the chance, because without that girl could find her way back he didn't have nothing but a few lumps of ore and a pile of hot air.

Charlie had never filed on this claim, hadn't staked it out or recorded it, either. This was not, on his part, either laziness or ignorance.

He guessed he was pretty ignorant, come right down to it. But he had known well enough the laws about claims and filing – sufficient anyway to want to keep clean away from them. The whole history of mining was crammed with litigations and the sad sad stories of guys like himself that had been jumped or frozen out.

To record his find – or so Charlie'd reckoned – would have been right down tantamount to handing Jones the means of taking it away from him. So long as the source of this ore stayed a mystery he had figured to be able to laugh at the man. But then that girl had come along half out of her noggin.

He'd had to stumble onto her and, because she'd seemed so young and helpless looking, he had let a natural pity get the upper hand of caution. After fetching her to the caves and getting her on her feet he had woke up one day to the fact that he was stuck with her.

This had never had any part in his plans and, in the increasing disquiet of their close proximity, spooked by her transparent attempts to maneuver him into double harness, he'd been led into making the mistake of his life.

He had thought getting rid of her would be worth half his horde; had been glad to give it to her and gladder still when she'd rose to the bait and took off with that paper. Now it looked like he had been a damn fool.

His head was filled with a hodgepodge of things laced through with worries and premonitions of disaster. And behind everything else, buried deep but far from quiet, was the sour and restive knowledge that, in brass tacks fact, he had actually been *afraid* to put this find on record.

He reckoned if anyone ever got wind of it they would count him ready for a string of spools for sure. And sometimes, down in the dumps, he would wonder if maybe this wasn't the horrible truth. In such a frame of mind one time he'd yanked out his six-shooter staring like a ninny for upwards of an hour before, with a snort, he'd come out of it enough to go hunt up his jug.

Just the same, by grab, this whole deal was peculiar – and not just the ore with them palish green streaks that was stacked up like firewood clean across the far wall of that bottommost cavern. Even the caves themselves wasn't like no others he had ever been into. They was enough, by God, to give a man the shakes coming onto them like he had!

That top one had looked natural enough, even with the cabin and its padlocked door – until he'd got inside and discovered that windlass with the rope rotted off it. It wasn't until he'd happened to peer into the hole that he had spotted the hidden ladder and, driven by curiosity, had fashioned a pitchpine torch and gingerly crept down the thing to have himself a look.

Three levels opened off that shaft; he had used up most of a day poking around, going through each one as he came to it. He'd had trouble with the ladders which were in bad shape and crudely made to begin with. The lashings which bound the rungs to the uprights had apparently been fashioned from strips of rawhide and some of these were rotten, letting go under his weight several times to scare him mightily.

The first and second levels beneath the cabin cave had been mostly given over to a series of chambers remindful of pictures he had seen of old castles, tiny dungeon-like cubicles hardly bigger than monks' cells with rusted chains bolted into the rocks and a stink coming off them that, while not exactly loud, wasn't anything a feller would care to sniff for very long.

As a matter of fact he hadn't been through either level again after his first trip down that bottom ladder. One gut-squeezing look in the light of his torch at the far wall of the cavern which composed the lowest opening, or lateral, had pretty near turned his legs weak as water.

Yellow, it was, like the three nearer walls but, unlike those, queer figures and out-landish designs had in some faroff time been daubed on it in red, possibly to conceal the presence there of plaster, and perhaps for a time it had. But now this was cracked and buckled with a great hole yawning just under the ceiling where the ore he'd fetched O'Toole had toppled to spill across the floor. That whole great wall was nothing but a fooler of plaster, five or six layers deep, layed up to hide the ore stacked like cordwood from floor to roof.

He had no way of guessing how long it had been there, but more was packed in behind the chunks that had fallen – at least two more stackings, and every bit of it jewelry rock!

Thinking back on it now as he watched the day brighten from gray to pink to fast-spreading gold, he felt reasonably sure what he'd got hold of was not, strictly speaking, a mine but hidden booty – buried plunder, and the federal government had laws about that.

Laws, if he could find a way around them, meant no more to Charlie Medders than they did to T.K. Jones. Laws was for other people; but nobody that had all his marbles was like to hand over a haul like this for any bunch of dang bureaucrats in Washington to squabble over. A man would *have* to be a fool to do a crazy thing like that!

Charlie, staring, cursed again. There was no sound of dogs, no sign of trackers. He had looked for Burks to have his Injuns out by this time. It didn't make sense Jones would let him get away without his greedy mind had fastened on something better; and the only thing Medders could think of was that stock-baited meeting the banker had called for one o'clock.

He clapped a hand to his brow, groaning aloud, reluctant to even consider going back, and yet... he couldn't stand the thought of being someplace else while the fate of what he had found was decided with no one to stand between himself and the poorhouse. Jones would pick him cleaner than a neck-wrung hen!

IX

Spurred by his apprehensions Medders got back to town well ahead of the meeting to find the streets seething in a froth of excitement. Slipping around to his room he stuffed into his pockets the rest of the cash he had got for his ore, caught up his pistol and then, by back alleys, hustled over to Fritchet's to pick up a sack of grain, just in case.

There was nobody around but the old man himself, half asleep in the shade on a tipped-back chair with his hat pulled over his face against flies.

"Well," he said, with a sour look at Charlie, "reckon you're off to join the stampede."

"What stampede?"

"Mean you ain't heard about them Injuns? Where the hell you been? Three diff'ent Papagos come in this mornin' with pieces of rock that was damn near pure silver. Whole town's gone loco! All the bar flies an' saddle tramps has took out for the mission with just about everything they

71

could steal, beg or borrow. Talk about commotion!"

Medders, grinning, said, "Musta been some of that stuff I pitched away."

"I guess it must've," Fritchet said dryly. Then his swung-about stare became sharply probing. "Didn't I hear you'd made some kinda strike?"

Medders sniffed. "What's the chances of pryin' you loose of a sack of that grain you got stacked yonder?"

"Cash or credit?"

"Didn't figure my credit was good around here."

"It ain't," Fritchet said, not bothering to get up. But he mighty near tipped over his chair when Medders tossed a gold piece into his lap. Eyeing it askance he came onto his feet. "One be enough?"

"One's plenty," Charlie grinned, "an' you kin keep the change."

The old man insisted on helping him load; but the story was different when he got to Sol Warner's adobe-fronted mercantile. The place looked like a cyclone had hit it. "No, you can't!" Warner snapped. "Lookit them shelves – body'd think I been host to a convention of locusts! Picks, shovels, blastin' powder – even cleaned me out of rice an' flour! Hmm . . . you're in luck," the merchant

72

grunted, peering into a limp sack. "Seems I've still got a pound or two left. Beans, I mean. You fixed t' tote 'em this way?"

He reached out the sack and Medders, taking it, paid him.

"Wouldn't be surprised if you run into a mite of wind," Warner said, considering him slanchways. "Town dads was lined up outside the bank –"

"*Was!*"

"That's right. Sent Burks around with a change of time and a fresh proposition. Said he'd buy up your debts at full ledger value or, if stock was voted, a man could have it in shares at four cents on the –"

But Medders, wild of eye, was already half across the street and moving faster with every leap.

He tore into the bank like a gust of brimstone, sent Brass Buttons sprawling; but hauled up, breathing hard, before Miss Winters' anxious smile.

"Gracious!" she said worriedly, her gentian glance darting up at the clock. "I think you'd better hurry. Mr. Jones held things up as long as he could ... Go right on in, Mr. Medders."

So it was *Mister* Medders now, Charlie noted, but was not to be softsoaped by titles and smiles. He went through the gate and

73

flung open Jones' door. Talk and the smoke of fifty cent cigars swirled around him like a wave as he strode into the crowd packed five deep about Jones' desk.

No one straightaway appeared to notice his presence and from the squabble of voices it was quickly apparent not all of this bunch was wholeheartedly happy with the way things were going. The banker's tones cut abruptly through the bickering gabble. "There you are, Mr. Tooper . . . forty-three dollars and sixty-four cents. Now," Jones said, clearing his throat and speaking briskly, "if there's nobody else who wants to settle for cash, those who have can depart and the rest of us will get down to the business in hand."

His glance, sliding through the disgruntled rumble of those going out, suddenly lit upon Medders and turned narrowly blank. But he was not easily put out of countenance. "Well, Charles," he said through the clomp of feet and departing mumble, "I see you finally managed to get here," and coldly smiled as he gathered up and began squaring the edges of a considerable batch of papers left on his desk by Medders' paid-off creditors.

"Didn't figure," Charlie said, "you could git very far without me."

Behind this brave front there was a dismal

wind blowing through his hopes as he eyed that bunch of bills in Jones' hands.

When Burks had got the leavers all herded from the room you could count the ones left and have fingers to spare. One was Burks himself who was lower, by Medders' reckoning, than the belly of a snake and had no more right to be among those present than a cow had with bloomers. It was plain Jones aimed for him to stay. The others – except the girl – were all persons of some consequence, like Ferris of Ores Amalgamated and old man Rawlins that owned the Boxed Bar T.

Jones got the meeting called to order and they all sat down in the chairs Burks fetched in, Ferris and Rawlins lighting up fresh smokes from the box passed around and then T.K., getting up behind his desk, put on his brightest smile. "All of us here know Charlie Medders, I guess, but you should also nod to Miss Belita Storn who, along with myself, has been one of Charles' partners in a rediscovered property from which these samples are fairly typical specimens. Mr. Burks will pass them around."

Medders didn't much care for a great deal of that – the "rediscovered" bit particularly – but chewed down on his tongue to listen in stony silence to the astonished exclamations that followed the rocks around. Ferris, as Burks took them back to their keeper, peered sharply at Charlie, but kept his notions to himself. Rawlins, concerned for his range, stared glumly at his boots. It was Heintzleman – a mortician who kept among his boxes a cheap sideline of household furnishings – that demanded to be told where the specimens had come from.

"Glad you brought that up, Abe. This is the ore fetched in by those Indians that sent half the town stampeding for the Santa Cruz." Jones grinned at their startled looks and chuckled. "Our associate, Mr. Medders, is a great hand for jokes. There's nothing around that mission, I assure you, that Charles has not deliberately put there. It will buy us, I think, whatever time we'll need to locate the main ore bodies and have them filed on in the name of the Company."

The grudging looks of respect sent Charlie's way by these words lifted Medders' head and thawed much of his antagonism, being the first of the kind he'd ever got from these wallopers. Then his glance fell on the girl, turning sour as he remembered the purpose of this meeting. It put his back up again, bunched the muscles in his cheeks.

Rawlins, rolling the smoke across his teeth,

grumbled, "How much capital will be needed to develop these claims?"

"We'll get to that presently. First thing we've got to do is form a company – we'd better have Miss Winters in," Jones said, pressing a buzzer. "Now, with regard to electing a head, unless someone has a better idea I think, inasmuch as this was Charles' discovery, it is certainly just and eminently proper he should be our first President – all in favor so signify by saying 'aye'."

"Aye!"

"Objection?"

Not a sound could be heard.

Medders, with his jaw hanging ludicrously open, was so completely astounded, so bewilderingly filled with the sanctified importance of so signal an honor being unanimously tendered by the town's mightiest moguls, that he was too choked up to speak.

Several of them grinned, two or three reached over to clap him on the back. Heintzleman, grabbing his fist, solemnly pumped it. By the time Charlie emerged from roseate visions and the enveloping warmth of brotherly love enough to become aware of what was going on, the company was formed and Miss Winters was reading back the names of those elected to hold office. Jones, it appeared, had been installed as Vice President. Heintzleman was Secretary, Rawlins was the Treasurer and Ferris, of Ores Amalgamated, was General Superintendent. An issue of preferred stock had been declared, of which each single share was to have a par value of one hundred dollars and they were ready now to vote as to whether or not common stock should be put on the market to finance development.

Medders, appalled, suddenly jumped to his feet. "Now just a dang minute! I dunno much about this business of stock, but –"

"I'll handle that end of it," Jones said smoothly. "All you have to do, Charles, is sit back and figure out some way to spend your profits. And that," the banker smiled, "should be occupation enough for even a man of your unbounded talent."

"Yeah. Well," Medders said, taking a long hard look at him, "I might not have got to the front row on figures but as President of this outfit I reckon I've got enough say to be heard."

"Certainly," Jones chuckled. "You go right ahead."

"Well, it's not goin' to cost all that much to git the ore out that we've got to come up with a stock sale t' do it."

"I'm surely relieved to hear that," Rawlins said, brightening somewhat.

"But the facts of the matter is," Ferris pointed out, "no big operation in this kind of thing ever figures to spend its own money on development." And Jones vigorously nodded. "It's not a business-like approach, and anyway," he added, mouth tightening around his smile, "it's not among the President's prerogatives to say how the Company's financial affairs –"

Medders said, interrupting: "I don't know much about company jobs, but it seems like a feller holdin' fifty percent of an outfit's shares would have considerable –"

"Let's not put the cart before the horse," Jones said. "The handling of stock is my department. I'm afraid you're out of order. Perhaps we had better deal with first things first." He looked around for the Board's approval.

Medders, leaning over the table, growled, "I go fer that. When you've got the stock ready to be passed out, hang your drawers in the winder an' we'll git together. Meetin' adjourned."

"Now see here," Jones cried, "we've had enough of your lip! You served your function when you uncovered this ore. Production – what we want and need now – requires abilities far beyond the scope and savvy of

79

any shirt-tail, single-blanket jackass prospector! You going to argue that?"

Medders, too, was up on his feet, looking nervous and uncertain, half inclined toward bluster. "Just the same," he growled stubbornly, "it seems like to me a guy with fifty percent of a company's holdings –"

"That's exactly the point. When the shares are passed out you won't have but twenty-five, the same as Miss Storn and myself."

Medders stared. "I guess," he said, "I better straighten you out. I might be soft in the head but I ain't that soft. The only part of this find that don't belong t' me is that half interest I –"

"Perhaps you're forgetting something." Jones, grabbing up the sheaf of papers he had clipped together, strode around his desk to shake them under Charlie's nose. "The receipted notes for those debts you run up – remember? The bank took them in to save the Company embarrassment, but you needn't imagine I'm going to absorb them.

"Ferris and Rawlins – and Heintzleman, too – are entitled to stock. When the shares are divided the bank will turn these back to you in exchange for your surplus twenty-five shares, which the bank will then turn over to these gentlemen for cash in the amount paid out on your debts."

80

While they stood like that, fiercely glaring at each other, Belita Storn, strangely pale in a wasp-waisted gown and feathered hat of burgundy velvet, sat twisting her hands with her eyes big as buckets.

Rawlins grinned, watching Charlie feel the turn of the screw. Even Ferris, though continuing to hold his face poker sober, must have counted those shares as good as tucked in his pocket.

"Go on," Medders grunted, "git the rest of it spit out."

A vague uneasiness tinged the banker's stare – a creep of puzzlement, too; but a glance at the girl appeared to bolster his faith, and again the sly smile commenced to tighten about his teeth. "That's it," he nodded. "That's all there is to it. Play square with us, turn over those shares, or explain to the court what went on out there between you and a child of Miss Storn's tender years, and how those chain scabs –"

Medders laughed. "Got it all figured out, eh?" He must have seen what a spot he was in, but "Go right ahead," he said, "an' see where it gits you. That jezebel's been dang handsome paid for whatever time she may have put in out there with me!"

"I think," Jones began, "when she tells her side of it –"

81

But Medders, already backing off, grinned sourly. "Sure, sure...be a lot of tears fall. Like to make me powerful hard to find, but don't you worry. When you've got your mine in that 'production' you mentioned just drop me a line an' I'll come right over. Meanwhile, I'm gittin' outa here – see?" and he banged one hand slapping down against his pistol.

Heintzleman cringed. The banker's face turned livid. Rawlins, under the malevolent stare, looked ready to dive for the protection of Jones' desk.

Medders openly sneered. "Them that stays put won't require lamentations." Waving derisively he ducked through the door.

X

There was obviously much Charlie Medders didn't know, but any kid in three-cornered pants could have sensed this was no time to be lingering in the environs of Tucson.

Jones would be after his scalp now for sure, and wouldn't much care how he lifted it, either, so long as it was probably the work of others and he could see in the offing any reasonable chance of subsequently turning up the source of Charlie's ore.

Swearing at his burros, Medders struck out once more toward the blue and gray shapes of the Tucson Mountains, pelting his charges with rocks to keep them humping. He was nursing no delusions as to how far Jones would go; about the only thing Charlie could find on his side was the certainty that, up to this point anyway, the banker could not know precisely where this horde was hidden.

But there was danger in the fact that Belita Storn had been there.

It didn't seem likely, by herself, that she could find her way back; but Jones and his cohorts, if they hadn't already, would soon worm out of her everything she could remember and, while in desert country one batch of hills looked pretty much like another, there were differences Apaches would have little trouble deciphering. Burks would have Injuns swarming all over, you could bet your old clay pipe on that.

He hadn't covered more than three-four miles when, scanning his backtrail from the vantage of a rise, he discovered dust and, eyes narrowing against the glare, presently made out the bent-forward shapes of three hard-riding horsebackers. They were hot on his tracks, no doubt about that. Without a glass he couldn't yet be sure of their identity, but the one in the lead had the build and look of Dry Camp Burks.

Medders, hotfooting after his burros, yanked loose his rifle from the ties of Begetta's pack and gave each of the beasts a double handful of grain while keeping one eye on the progress of the trio bent on running him to earth. If this were Burks, as he suspected, it was plain enough by the fact he'd fetched help the bank's removal expert wasn't taking this pasear just to exercise his horse.

They came on methodically, riding a high trot, quite apparently indifferent to Charlie's warlike preparations. About a mile away they broke apart, one cutting around to the north, one canting off into the south, the other – obviously Burks – keeping straight on. But just out of rifle range he stopped and swung down, watching his helpers completing their surround.

Medders, jacking a cartridge into the firing position, rested his rifle across the shelf of a boulder, adjusted his sights and settled back to wait.

Though matters more urgent nagged and scratched for his attention, Belita Storn in her fancy duds came big-eyed into his thinking, almost seeming as he recalled her now to be less than plumb happy with the turn things were taking. Probably regretting having brought such a grasper into this deal. She would not be the first to find Jones' charm wearing thin on closer acquaintance.

The demands of greed were hard to abide and the influence of power, with all its concomitant wants and drives, an abomination no real man could stomach; and the banker, at least by Charlie's lights, was no exception to this deplorable pattern. Every jasper within reach of his voice was expected, even compelled, to do precisely as T.K. ordered. Without you were a Rawlins or Ferris there was no other way to get along with the bugger. He was not the kind to tolerate free thought. You were for him or against him, and those who fell into the latter slot could expect short shrift and some pretty rough going.

Medders, baring his teeth, squeezed off a shot and watched Burks jump. He put his second slug closer, the third right on him. Then he dumped the pack off Begetta, scrambled onto her back and, as Jones' hardcase fled, went larruping after him. Time he got down onto the bottoms, however, Burks was just a departing dust.

Charlie watched that dust tear off east and pulled up, disgusted. There was no point running the hoofs off Begetta. To hell with a man that wouldn't stand and fight!

He peered around for the others, found they'd ducked out of sight like the coyotes they were. It was the way of their kind, hit and run, strike only when terrain and opportunity favored. Like a Injun – and maybe, by godfreys, that's what they were! Now he come to think of it, that one who'd cut south might have been old Pantsless Pete, the Papago tracker.

There was a way to find out, if you could lure him into it.

Turning back, Medders heeled Begetta up the ridge where Begat stood watch over the thrown-down pack. Getting off, Charlie replaced it and then, still toting his rifle, hazed both animals into a little known trail you'd have hardly believed even a goat could climb. These were slippery rocks scoured smooth by sand laden winds off the desert with a cliff to one side and fearful drops off the other. Someway the burros' sharp shod hoofs found purchase and Charlie, hanging on to Begat's stubby tail, was pulled along with them, sweating and cursing, shuddering each time a chunk of loose shale went clattering down out of sight far below.

By hard work Medders looked to rim out before dark. If Burks & Company didn't come sneaking after him Charlie figured to throw a circle and strike off for the cave across a windy stretch that by morning would show no more sign than a fly would leave on a crust of dry bread. Hell, why take chances with this bunch of drygulchers when his ore could be sold just as easy at Yuma or Phoenix!

It was well after six when they came out on a crest of bald rock and Medders, digging the glass from his pack, squatted down for a long careful look. He could see from this vantage San Xavier del Bac and considerable activity between the gypsum white of its structures and the tree-fringed gorge of the Santa Cruz where that bunch of Tucson loafers were busily gophering up the ground. Off to the north another spread of dust was inching along the Ajo trail bound straight for the granite-ribbed slopes of this very peak, and it was not being raised by any two-three hombres.

Bitterly counting dots, near as Charlie could figure there was upwards of fifteen rannies down there slicking leather – a heap too many to be anything but a posse. And there was just one answer to that. Jones had given his sheriff orders to fetch Medders in.

After another ten minutes of trying to locate Burks and that pair he had with him, it came over Charlie suddenly their whole purpose in being out here could be to effect a surround and drive him into the arms of McFarron's deputies.

If this were true he had given that black-haired pair time enough to get through and be waiting to pick him up when he came out of the rocks, which he would have to do if he was minded to cross the Altar Valley, his original intention. The hills he was bound for were hidden from here, west and somewhat south, beyond the Baboquivaries, all Papago country, rough and wild as a javalina.

He could work north from here – if Burks didn't spot him – and drop down into the Avra Valley, another arid stretch fifty miles off his course, and from there, swinging south around the Roskruge Mountains, reach the cave – if him or the burros didn't give out first. But there was no water that way, and the big fly here was the whereabouts of Burks. It didn't have to follow that because he couldn't spot Burks the bank's trouble-shooter was under a like handicap. The ugly son of a bitch could be watching right now!

It wasn't enough they had stolen his ore, glommed onto that four hundred and more of O'Toole stingy cash he'd been forced to pitch into the banker's hat – they had to whipsaw him out of the whole shebang and, when that hadn't worked, drive him into the rocks!

Fury yanked back his lips in the snarl of a cougar. If it was fight they wanted he would give them a bellyful!

Reloading his rifle, the sixteen pound Sharps that could knock a man kicking at a thousand yards, he sent Begat and Begetta grumbling over the divide and in a lathering froth of self pity and outrage started recklessly down the mountain's far side, muttering and mumbling like a pulque drunk squaw.

These tumbled west slopes – blood red in the rays of the near-vanished sun, the top rind of which still thrust a lighthouse arc across the jagged scarp of Dobbs Buttes towering above the far sea of the desert's darkening floor – were but lightly clad with a gnarled growth's stubble, offering only sporadic chances of concealment. But Charlie, in a mood to welcome violence, pressed on uncaring as a prodded bull.

The rocks over here were still hot to the touch, sun glare flittering and flashing from their slants, the roasted air still as stove lids. If they were over here they would probably spot him – there was just this one trail down from where he'd been. There was no good grousing at what couldn't be helped. You couldn't hide the clop and clatter. The big thing now was to get into the sand drifts where he had some prospect of losing the banker's minions and where, once night fell, no glass could spy him out.

The roundabout brush and rocks turned blue-gray as the sun fell suddenly behind black buttes and, partway down, Medders stopped long enough at a cliffside seep pawed from the shale by mountain wildlife to let his burros tank up while he threw off their packs, afterwards letting them roll and stretch before, reloading, he again choused them on.

He kept sharp watch but in the curdle of shadows found nothing to alarm him. That posse, ere now, had likely got through the pass, but it wasn't McFarron's crowd that bothered him. They'd be just average fellers that could be scraped up anyplace, counter jumpers and maybe a merchant or two, pieced out with whatever ranch hands had happened to be available. It was the whereabouts of Burks and his two long-haired partners that was keeping Charlie's hide filled with prickles and itchings. Them was the kind a man had to look out for.

Still raking the gloom with hard stabs of his glance Medders followed his charges off the last shelves of detritus and on toward the final outcrops of rock that, here, toadlike crouched against the darkening night.

The wind was coming up now, whistling in off the desert. It would be good to get back and hole-up in his cave; and he was able to let down a little just thinking of it. This being keyed up all the time was no good. Be smarter, probably, to leave the damned ore where it was and keep riding; and if he hadn't been crowded so much maybe he would have, he told Begetta, watching her flop her ears in the dark. But it was too late for that. To ride off now, after the way he'd been treated, was more than a man of spirit could abide, knuckling under to a bunch of paid gunnies, tucking his tail like the rest of these yahoos every time Jones saw fit to stamp a boot. *Somebody* had to take a stand against those buggers!

With Begat in the lead and Charlie tugging the fractious Begetta – knee deep in the tantrum she generally threw whenever she was hungry or worked beyond her quota – they forged into the gale with nothing beyond that last reef of rock but the dark and wind-tossed wastes of the desert.

Begat, abruptly snorting, threw up his
91

head and whistled like an elk. About to whirl he coughed and dropped. Medders, ducking, heard the crack of a rifle. Begetta, tail up, went past like a cat streaking over a tin roof as Charlie, palming his six-shooter, emptied it about him and, yelling like a Comanche, took to his heels.

XI

That blast of wild fire he'd flung into the night may well have been all that saved Charlie's bacon. At least it had pinned the bushwhackers down for what time he'd used getting past those rocks and into the wind driven howl of the desert.

A man had to fight just to catch his breath in the swirl of grit whipped up off these drifts, but there was this much about it: in this screaming dark that was thicker than gar soup laced with tadpoles no one was going to match him up with a bullet without he got turned around and went blundering into them. Or into those horsebackers McFarron had hunting him.

He hated losing Begat, but he hadn't much time to get worked up about it, having all he

92

could do to keep hold of Begetta. Now that her recent fright was forgotten the great bulk of her energy was being devoted to displaying her displeasure. She didn't *like* being hauled into the teeth of such a gale, did everything she could to make Charlie's progress as difficult as possible, twisting and jerking, grunting and trying to plant her feet against his intention – even so, finally, practically sitting on her haunches. Which was when, fed to the gills, Medders went for her with the rope's end.

Snorting with surprise the startled burro sprang erect in considerable haste. *Prowww!* she exclaimed in unmistakable outrage. But when her master, with peeled-back lips, shook out his rope she stood not upon the order of her going but, with gritted teeth and tucked-in tail, went stomping ahead with flattened ears.

Bucking the scour of those sandblasting gusts was no joke in all conscience, but it was better than a bullet, Medders figured, wallowing after her. And a hell of a sight better than being forced to choose between surrendering the location of his cache or going to jail on the trumped-up charges of that ungrateful jezebel – her and that banker! There was two of a kind for you!

He found it hard to understand people like

that. Ready to do anything, just so it showed a profit!

He pushed along with what speed he could, knowing from much experience of this region the worst of the blow probably wouldn't last much over a couple of hours. The more ground they could cover before beginning to leave tracks the better. In fact, Charlie concluded after much weighing of possible courses, it might turn out to be smarter not to head for the cave.

Crossing this stretch of the Avra was likely to take the best part of the night and no guarantee of being under cover then. Once the sun got up, and with no sand blowing, it might be possible with a glass for someone back there in the mountains to get a line on them – just to catch a flash of movement would be all a guy sharp as Burks would need.

Deciding he'd best not risk it, Medders let Begetta drift a bit to the left, more into the east if there'd been any east to see. This allowed her to feel she was putting something over; it threw the wind on their flank, making for faster and easier travel.

The valley was narrower off in that quarter. In addition to offering a shorter trek to cover, it held the added attraction of dropping any sign they might eventually leave in a region Burks and his redskins could prowl to their hearts' content.

Might even carry them to Sombrero Butte or, beyond, up into the Twin Buttes country, which was all right with Charlie. This was south of the mission, and he knew for a fact there was considerable float all through those hills.

Burks might very well pick up some chunks, wedding him to the natural and erroneous conviction he was hot on the trail of his quarry's hidden lode. While the hue and cry was raging off there Charlie and Begetta, having swung west again, could be following the San Juan, later dropping south to slip through the Baboquivaries and move leisurely north up their western flanks to come at his cache without one chance in a hundred of tipping their hand.

The only risk was water. They'd be cooked sure enough if they couldn't find water. But in mountain country, if you knew what to look for, you nearly always could. He wasn't worried about that; in fact, the prospect was so pleasing he had a couple good belly laughs picturing Burks and those poor damn Injuns.

The wind continued vigorously to pummel, lash and tug at them. He had never known it so belligerent or persistent. Once,

95

slapped out of his thoughts by its fury, he found it nipping at his heels. This time, alarmed, he lit into Begetta with the lead shank as well. "Just like a goddam woman!" he railed. "How many times does a jasper have t' tell you?" He raised his voice in a yell. "You go shyin' off again, by grab, I'll put you straight into it!" He gave her another taste of the rope and climbed onto her then to make sure she remembered.

Perhaps he dozed. Next thing he knew – at least the next time he noticed – she was stone-still stopped and peering back at him reproachful.

Medders jerked up his head.

The damn wind had quit. He guessed it was still short of morning but nowhere near as dark as it had been – nor was this all. He could remember closing his eyes against the grit but he could not recall any slackening of the gale. There was something just ahead, looming up through the murk like... well, it *looked* like a wall... probably a cliff or a butte. Begetta had apparently pulled into the lee....

He looked again, legs clamping.

It *was* a wall. With a kind of sick horror it came over him he was staring at the rear of Fritchet's stable. He was back in

96

town! Turned around by that storm he had come full circle.

XII

Mighty infrequent had the buffetings of fate ever caught Charlie Medders without some kind of comeback; but, honest to John, the crumpling weight of this latest disaster sat so heavily on him he could not even cuss.

He couldn't stay here. And no one but a idjit would think to head back into that desert, crawling like it was with T.K. deputies and gunslingers.

Clutched by panic, held fast by facts, Medders hunkered there gulping like a buzzard too gorged to get off the ground.

There were other ways open – he didn't *have* to head west. Off north were the Santa Catalinas and, beyond, still more mountains. Northeast were the Rincons and Galiuros and, straightout east, the Dragoons, Winchesters and Dos Gabezas. There was no lack of hideouts if a man could reach them.

Stepping back he stood bitterly consider-ing Begetta. Her spraddle-legged stance
97

showed how far he'd get on *her;* and that stack of grain he'd bought off Fritchet had someway got torn open and was now plastered to her like a wrung-out rag. If he could get a horse from Fritchet...

He thrust a hand in his pocket and groaned. The weight of what coins he'd departed this town with had brought on a hole, and past experience with the liveryman did not encourage pinning hope on credit.

A search of his other pockets turned up one crumpled handkerchief, twenty-five hand-loaded shells for the Sharps and eight pistol cartridges for the shot-dry gun tucked into his waistband.

And it was getting light fast.

He stripped his gear off Begetta and turned her loose. She didn't move from her tracks, just huddled there, head hanging, looking woebegone and friendless as Charlie felt himself.

They had sure as hell come to a fine pass, he thought. Glaring about wildly, he wondered if he could slip back up to his room.

A dog barked somewhere while Charlie, cringing, desperately dredged up the names of his most likely acquaintances. There wasn't one he could think of who might cross up Jones to help him.

He edged along the wall as breath-held and fluttery as though at any moment he figured to step on a cat, hoping the stable's back door had not been fastened. But, arrived before it in the graying gloom, envisioning the uproar that would be loosed if he were discovered, try as he would he couldn't bring himself to touch it. There were horses in some of those pens off yonder but Fritchet was the kind who slept with one eye open and a sawed-off at his elbow.

It was plain he had to do something, and quick. going to be plumb light inside another half hour. If he hadn't squeezed into some hole before then he could wind up dead in the trash of some alley.

It wasn't Burks so much that he was scared of now but the crazy damn talk that would be flying around about him feuding with Jones, and the way McFarron's posse would sure as hell come into this. Be plenty of trigger-happy jaspers around that might think to curry favor by knocking him off. Guys had turned up dead before in this town!

He wasn't at all keen for stepping out into that street. He took a good look first, up one side and down the other, not liking any part of it. Next door there were two vacant lots or maybe three; beyond, however, both sides were packed solid, buildings cheek by jowl and even closer, business establishments all the way clean to Main where the bank's watchtower turret starkly rose above the town's false fronts.

Tucson's climate rarely produced mist but the curdled shadows, like dirty fleece, seemed to crawl in weaving swirls and stringers, almost alive. Every open place was choked with the stuff – thin like smoke writhing away as a man advanced. Like a mirage, Charlie thought, nervously shivering in this pre-dawn gloom.

Shoulders hunched and hat pulled low he struck off obliquely across the vacant lots, aiming behind these marts of trade to come into the back streets given over to homes, hoping among such countrified parts to come onto some empty house or barn. If he could just find somewhere to drop out of sight till night came again to enlarge his chances. . . .

At least these places had more space between them, but it was graying up faster with each passing moment. He was two streets over from Fritchet's already and no sign of anything a man might crawl into. He didn't dare run. There was a barn up ahead with weeds grown around it and a couple of boards off the side that looked enough abandoned to maybe make do.

He swerved toward it, then stopped. He scrubbed the sweat from his eyes and peered again at the house and fence beyond. A white and green frame, newly painted by the look; something about it tugging fierce but calling up nothing he could put a finger on. Still toting the Sharps he stepped gingerly into the barn's musty dark, thankful he didn't have to hunt for a door.

It was quiet in here as a tubful of grass and Charlie stood, stiff with listening waiting for his eyes to grow adjusted to the gloom. Something moving outside was snuffling around in the weeds. Clamped to his rifle Charlie stood without breathing, expecting any moment to be discovered. But no alarms exploded, no shout went up. It got so still he could hear his goddam heart.

The place was thick with dust and cobwebs. Old lumber lay stacked in one corner, gray and bowed with time and warp. Three box stalls, empty except for tatters of straw, and on the far side a great closed door and a closed smaller one built into one corner. Several scraps of rusty harness hung from pegs against one wall. Two lengths of baled hay lay gray with dust and folds of spider web near the middle of this ram-shackle shell. Charlie finally moved over, gingerly perched on one of them, cradling the Sharps across his lap.

"Well!" a female voice said abruptly. "What are *you* doing here?"

Medders, jerked to his feet, peered apprehensively about. Neither door had been opened. Not a soul was in sight, but through the hole in the siding he could see gray sand and the green of weeds; by this he knew another morning had begun. But all remained so quiet he began presently to wonder if he had really heard the words or, dozing, only imagined them.

He was not long in doubt. "Come on, now... I'm not going to hurt you," she coaxed.

Charlie's glance stabbed wildly at the barn's four corners, from their obscurity skittering panicky to the place in the wall where the boards had fallen off. Begetta, ears cocked, stood peering in and back of her, coolly considering him across the burro's tawny shoulders, was the inscrutably handsome face of Miss Winters.

Medders loosed a shaky sigh. He understood now what had gripped him outside when he'd spotted that house with its white picket fence – the old Winters place that her father had left before he'd shuffled off and

102

Imogene, to feed herself, had gone to work in Jones' bank as private scribe and sweet-talking watchdog to the man's inner sanctum.

While they stared at each other through the stickery stillness Charlie reckoned he could hardly have gotten deeper into the fat had he camped on the doorstep of T.K. himself. With Jones, at least, he could have put up a scrap, but faced with the elegant Imogene Winters a guy was tied to the mast, left not even the solace of swearing.

"I rather imagined you were in there," she said. "What really eludes me is what you thought... Well! The whole town knows Begetta. If you were hoping to hide –"

"How'd I know the dang fool was out there! I expect," Charlie growled, "you're goin' to have to turn me in?"

"All those men... it *is* a bit expensive. What would you suggest?"

Medders' jaw fell open. Miss Winters smiled and, when his look turned suspicious, loosed a tinkle of silvery laughter. "I suppose you are feeling pretty sorry for yourself. You mustn't judge everyone in the light of T.K. You did make him look pretty silly, you know."

"You mean..." Charlie swallowed like he doubted his hearing.

103

"He is pretty worked up over you, I'll admit." She stood silent then, lips slightly parted, tip of pink tongue thoughtfully crossing the lower one. "Actually, you've no need to hide out –"

"No need!" Charlie gasped. "What about Burks an' them Injuns! An' that dadburned posse!"

She said, "Perhaps I'd better get under cover," and stepped out of his sight. Before he could gather enough spit to swear, the smaller door opened and she came into the barn, Begetta rather gingerly stepping in after her. "Burks and those deputies were just to keep you hopping around until he has this business fully organized and rolling."

Charlie couldn't peg that, was so mixed up by this time he couldn't have recognized dung from wild honey. He stood there goggling like he was short on his marbles count. "You mind trampin' that trail again?"

"The new venture," she said. "The company they've organized to exploit your find. I'd no idea there was so much to do ... machinery to be bought and transported, drills, blasting powder – such a miscellany of equipment. We were all there working till almost one o'clock last

104

night. I would never have guessed a mine required –"

"But there *ain't* no mine!" Medders cried, exasperated. "Alls I've got . . ."

Her smile cut him off. "You can't keep a thing big as this off the street – T.K. said so himself. The whole town was in an uproar, especially after Father Eusebio told us those pieces of ore his Papagos brought in were chunks you'd thrown trying to scare your burros out of his corn." She said as though it were a pity: "T.K., of course, had to give it to the papers. I suppose by now they've put the story on the wire –"

"*What* story?"

She peered at him, astonished. "Why . . . about you uncovering the old Weeping Widow that's been lost all these years. Well, he had to tell them *something,*" she declared with a flash of defiance for what she saw in his face.

Her look changed, though, when Medders, flinging down his hat, began to guffaw like a loony. "Is that what he told 'em? That I found the Weepin' Widder?"

Mis Winters' eyes seemed a little uneasy. "You *did* find it, didn't you?"

"Hell, no! Alls I've got is a cache of stacked ore some bunch of highgraders went an' buried in a cave!"

Miss Winters cringed as though she'd been struck; but whether this was caused by his language or its import was not apparent. With shock still in her stare she said, rising determinedly above it: "T.K. had your number, all right. He said you would try to upset everything. But they've allowed for your spleen – this dog in the manger attitude. Once the operation is down on the books it will be money in the bank no matter how loud you shout."

"Got it all figured, hey?"

She considered him belligerently. "T.K. believes in the fact accomplished. You're not the first desert rat he's been involved with; he knows how obstinate and unreasonable prospectors can be, always stirring up trouble, haggling over every move."

She seemed to catch herself, drew a long shaky breath. "I shouldn't be talking like this . . . I can't think what has come over me." She caught a lip between white teeth, eyes nearly hidden behind the cover of dark lashes. "Practically *trading* with the enemy."

Medders got the message. "Ever think of swappin' sides?"

"But wouldn't that be disloyal?" Her eyes seemed suddenly big as buckets. "I mean,

106

a girl does have to look out for herself, but..."

"Shucks," Charlie said, "there ain't no buts about it. *You* ought t' know how these big moguls operate. In business today it's every wolf fer himself." He let her digest that, then said quick and easy: "Be worth a little somethin' fer me t' know what's in them minutes. After all, I guess you could say I *founded* the Company. I got a right t'know, ain't I?"

"Well, but..."

She was plainly wavering. "Miss Winters –" he broke off.

A timid, half scared bit of smile was on her lips. "W-wouldn't you rather call me 'Ginnie'?"

Medders noticeably gulped. But a man had to strike while the iron was hot. Clambering over his alarm he grumbled, "You bet...Ginnie. Now, look...as the duly elected boss of this outfit I oughta know what was decided after I walked out – I wanta see them minutes."

"They're locked in the safe."

"You took notes, didn't you?"

She said, shaking her head: "T.K. wouldn't like it."

"How's he goin' t' find out?"

She searched his face, dubious. Charlie

patted her shoulder. For a clincher he said, "If there was somethin' you liked an' I could manage t' git it..." and grinned at her, waiting.

She stood twisting her fingers and, not looking at him, blurted: "A s-share in the C-Company?"

Charlie's grin got a little brittle.

What the hell! he told himself. If it came to a vote he was up the crick anyway if Jones went ahead and split this up like he'd threatened. A feller needed to know what that scissorbill was up to, somebody on the inside to *keep* him in the know. These shares didn't mean a goddam thing without that bunch found out where the ore was. And he sure wasn't about to tell anyone that!

He gave her the nod. While she scooted to the house to fetch her squiggles he cast up in his head the percentages Jones had pushed as a basis for dividing up the Company shares. Belita, Jones and Charlie, it appeared, would account in equal amounts for 75% of the Company's control, the remaining 25 to be distributed between Ferris, Rawlins and that bootlicking Heintzleman.

If that was the way it was going to be sliced, another share more or less wouldn't make any difference. A blind mule could see he was already staring down the throat of the

108

gun, his equity whittled to a measly quarter interest, and no say at all when it came to setting up policy. As general superintendent Ferris would be in charge of production which, in actual practice, would mean the whole works – cave, ore, and all the rest of the tangible assets, with Jones in control and Medders, who had made it all possible, nothing but a name at the top of the sheet.

It was enough to cramp rats; but, wild as it was, Charlie still held the joker – the hugged-closed knowledge of the source of the ore on which this whole deal was predicated. He didn't see how they were going to get around that and, bad debts or no, it was a pretty big stick – the club he figured would get back his fifty percent.

So when Miss Winters returned with her book of notes, rather than admit his backwardness at reading, he found a blank page, handed the book back, and told her to dash off an order on the Company instructing Jones to turn over one share of Medders' interest in said Company to her, after which he took the pencil and laboriously scrawled his name.

"Now," he said, sleeving the sweat off his cheeks, "you flip through them laundry marks an' say what's been done. Just the facts – never mind the whereases an' wherefores."

It took them ten minutes to get through the orders for miscellaneous equipment, the gangs to handle it and put down a road, the drilling and mucking, timbering, hauling, and the staggering maze of detailed other services projected by the quorum of Board members Charlie had walked out on. Then the shares were brought up and passed out to those present, and right about there Medders lunged to his feet.

"Passed out!" he shouted, grabbing off his hat. "Hell's fire – how *could* they? Ain't been enough time even to hev any *printed!*" and he glared so fierce Imogene shrank back, eyes like scorched holes in the bedsheet pallor of her pulled-tight cheeks.

Yet it was not fright which made her peer at him so – or perhaps it was, a little. Mostly, however, this was caused by distaste, a patrician repugnance for the crudity of him, his offensive language, the reckless ever-churning tendency she felt in him toward violence.

To all of these she was bitterly opposed, by rearing and environment as well as natural inclination; and, despite the willowy, sweet-smelling daintiness of figure and presence for which the bank had hired her, she had

110

that hard core of stubbornness which comes of handling facts.

Looking down her nose she said clearly and sharply: "You are wrong about that. T.K.'s been way ahead of you. The share certificates, needing only the signature of the Secretary Treasurer, were already printed and in the drawer of his desk when you left in such a dudgeon. Anticipating your reaction, knowing the Board would almost certainly approve the floating of a stock issue to be sold the general public, it may astonish you to know he had those ready, too; they'll be offered through the Exchange as soon as the wire service stories have encouraged a proper demand."

Like the kiss of death her smile curled around him: and then, still hugging her notebook with the page he had stupidly signed, she was gone.

XIII

It took several moments for Medders to realize the implications wrapped up in her disclosures. What he grasped straightaway was that once again the banker had got the best of him. It wasn't until he'd gone over her remarks the third or fourth time that he began to glimpse the full scope of T.K.'s triumph. It came over Charlie then how neat he'd been set up to catch the whole blame and direst penalties of the law if this swindle they were launching ever happened to get caught up with.

That it *was* a swindle he could no longer doubt. Jones had been so anxious to get that stock on the market he'd had the certificates printed before the Company was organized. He hadn't cared a snap of the fingers whether what Charlie'd found was a mine or just another damn hole in the ground. All he'd actually needed was those four sacks of ore Charlie'd sold O'Toole, and that court order he'd had McFarron serve, impounding them, had given him ready access. By now they were probably being shipped in dribbles and dabs all over the goddam country, specimens to tie in with those rushed-to-press stories crediting Medders with rediscovering the fabulous Weeping Widow all the feather-brains had been hunting for upwards of who knew how long! Then Jones had made him head of the Company so his name, as president, could be plastered on all the come-ons and letterheads!

Jones sure enough had him by the short

hairs this time. It was the worst damn bind he had ever stumbled into; and when his assessment of the situation reached this conclusion he took the route of panic, jumped aboard his burro and, before the hour was out, was flogging Begetta deep into the raging winds of the desert

This was wild rough country with nobody in it but coyotes and jackrabbits, tarantulas, scorpions and suchlike, but he still had his Sharps tight-clenched in his hand and was of a mind now to use it on the first two-legged varmint that showed.

He was through with towns. A honest man didn't have no more chance than a snowball in hell trying to abide by Christian principles among the scribes and Pharisees you found in control of the marts of trade. Out here a man had a halfway chance, and a gun made everyone equal.

Medders lost himself in the heart of the storm and when it blew itself out his mind was made up. Jones and his stooges had rigged the deck. With his name and his ore they had everything stacked to make a big killing. All that machinery and other equipment so brazenly detailed in the Company minutes didn't mean that they had it or ever would – except on paper. It would make a prospectus look awfully good to the widows and orphans and the rest of the suckers.

Hell! nobody had appointed Charlie their keeper. He was through batting *his* head against a stone wall! He peered around, got his bearings, and struck off north, hauling Begetta drag-footed after him. He had two big cans of water buried close and, soon as the moon got properly up, he reckoned to find them. It was all right to talk, but deep in his bones Medders knew mighty well he had not yet heard the last of that banker.

No matter how much they grossed with their fraudulent stock, Jones and his cohorts would never be satisfied. They would always be wondering if he *did* have a mine, and sooner or later they'd take steps to find out.

Well, a man had no recourse against such vultures in town, but out here things were different. A good man with a rifle could get a run for his money.

Let 'em bring on their Injuns! Nobody knew this wild country like he did. He could live off land where them town sports would starve, and one of these times – soon's he got around to it – he'd take off a few days and put in some more of these tin-can springs . . . just in case.

As for that swivel-hipped Ginnie, she

114

could have her share and welcome. The more he saw of women, by grab, the better he liked their four-legged sisters. With a burro a man knew where he was at, but a woman was just another name for trouble.

And he went grumbling on, swearing and snarling at the way he'd been taken, telling himself that if he had it to do over he'd have emptied some hats before he lit out. And he would sure as hell do it if any of that bunch ever got up the nerve to come snooping around!

He spent a cold night with nothing to put over him or inside his belly. Begetta wasn't partial to it, either, and was not averse to letting him know it. He finally had to tear a couple strips from his shirt tail and stuff them in his ears before he could get any sleep.

It was well after six when the dadburned critter, egged on no doubt by her empty gut, nuzzled him out of his uneasy dreams. Sore eyed and tousled from his bout with the winds Charlie, aching and miserable, pushed up with a curse.

He took a long look around. Then, hawking and spitting, he sluiced out his throat from the can they'd dug up, took a grimacing swig for the good of his tapeworm, gurgled some into his hat for Begetta, reburied the rest and caught up his rifle. Squinting again over the far swell of drifts he gave Begetta the nod and, with a scowl for the scoured-clean brightness of the day, morosely struck out after her.

Inside two hours it was uncomfortably hot. Before mid-morning they were out of the wind belt and into a region of sparse vegetation, none of it tall enough to throw any shade – greasewood and yucca, patches of prickly pear, Spanish dagger spikes. He peeled a few purple pears that were bitter enough to pucker a pig's mouth. He offered some to Begetta, watched her lip them suspiciously, make a horrible face and go snorting away. He managed to get down the rest of them himself after knocking out the seeds, but as a breakfast he found them pretty puny for a fact.

Distant hills began to shimmer and writhe in the furnace-dry heat, the mountains behind them turning gray as smoke through the interlacing film. The glare became ferocious; but three hours past noon wolf's candle appeared with its thorny gray wands and occasional vermillion blossom, and sparse clumps of grass began to fringe the climbing swells. Soon they were in better country, following a draw up into higher ground; the yucca fell behind and stunted

116

mesquites began to rear their gnarled trunks. Begeta, with quickening steps, was already crossing a spur up ahead before Medders spotted the outcrop he'd been hunting.

Now he could hear the burro scrambling up his private trail. The way rose slowly and with deceptive ease, but after the first bench it struck a steeper pitch, and from there on up it became one sharper slant piled on top of another. And there was wind up here among these treacherous rocks, sharp sudden gusts that could slam a man straight out into space. He gained another bench, somewhat better than halfway up and, tottering into the lee of a house-sized boulder, flopped down to rest, too goddam beat to go another foot.

But presently, after his muscles quit jumping and he got back some of his breath, he pulled himself up and took another long glower out over the country they'd just crawled out of. And again he cursed Jones, thinking bitterly of Begat and the loss of his glass, and of three or four things he would like to see happen to Dry Camp Burks.

So far as he could see there was no sign of pursuit. Now that T.K. had things going his way he had probably called off his gun thrower and ordered McFarron's posse home.

Still muttering and mumbling Medders
117

resumed the climb to his cave. He'd take another look there, but he guessed – for a while at least – he could let down a little and not expect every moment to have to cut and run or be ducking a blue whistler. Nothing wore a man down quicker than that kind of thing, and except for the way it would have made him look he might have seriously considered packing up and pulling out. No damned ore, not even silver rich as this, was worth getting killed for!

But next morning things looked different. Food and a good night's sleep had driven most of the daunsiness out of him. Whistling cheerfully, he fried up a breakfast of sow belly liberally seasoned with frijoles and chili peppers which he afterwards washed down with java hot from the can in which he had boiled it, strong enough to float a he-kangaroo.

He further relaxed in the fragrance of Durham and, when this was finished, climbed up to the cave mouth where, concealed by a tangle of manzanita, he considered again the dun miles spread below. His perch looked over some real desolation, a vast panorama of sunlit sand, here and there dappled by the dark thrust of mountains. But, pick and pry as he would and did, his hawklike stare could not raise

118

one dust that was not stirred by some vagary of wind. It was a peaceful scene, quiet as two six-shooters in the same belt.

He got up presently, climbed around some more rocks and peered down into the wild hay trap. Having satisfied himself he need have no worries about Begetta, who was dozing hipshot in the shade of a beanless mesquite, he went back in the cave, dug up a spare candle, put on his miner's cap and began a cautious descent of the reinforced ladders which brought him, after some seven or eight minutes, into the chamber where he'd found that cache of what he still considered to be stolen highgrade.

He got a hammer from his pocket and walked around tapping walls. Every blow rang solid. He found no evidence at all that might indicate even the remotest possibility of blocked-up passages or other hidden hoards. He would have liked to believe this *was* an old Spanish mine, but it seemed pretty obvious it was nothing of the sort.

He knocked loose more ore from the place he'd got the rest of it, digging back of what was already exposed to uncover another layer of equally rich specimens. But when, excited, he lifted several of these out in the hope there might be more, all he found for the bother was a wall of solid granite. Though he

119

widened the hole to a full yard across, each chunk removed uncovered nothing but more granite. The ore had not been extracted from that. It wasn't even the same color.

Medders, however, being human, was disappointed. That talk Jones had started kept gnawing at his thinking like a pack of hungry rats. Common sense told him the talk was nothing but sucker bait, part of that bunk T.K. had fed to the papers to stimulate demand for the worthless stock they proposed to foist on the public. Just the same he reckoned, peering cynically around, another pasear along those echoing corridors in the number 2 and 3 levels should settle the matter one way or the other.

He took another hard look at that torn-open wall. Three layers of this kind of stuff from floor to ceiling – even at the prices you had to take from a fence – wasn't nothing to be sneezed at. Well over a hundred thousand dollars' worth for certain.

Returning to the well shaft he started up the ladder. Peering into the blackness of that number 3 level he stood a while, scowling, remembering that series of tiny dungeon-like cubicles with the rusted chains bolted into the rock and the stink swirling round that made a man want to puke. He wasn't at all sure he cared to prowl the length of them again. Yet he hated to think of settling for the ore already stacked if there was any chance of this being a mine.

He left the shaft, reluctantly advancing into the black horror of this noisome passage whose shadows gave way like cornered beasts before the sizzling carbide arc of his lamp. Pistol gripped in sweaty palm, ears stretched, mouth breathlessly open, Charlie shuddered to a stop beside the first cell he came to. He knew from memory they were all alike, open faced and bare, yet forced his jumpety nerves to go on and so arrived, as he had that other time at gallery's end, against the same rough surface of cinnamon rock.

Crouched there, peering, he did a sudden double take.

This wasn't granite! Reaching out he touched the wall's raspy feel, backing hastily off to swap the pistol into his other hand while directing the lamp on his twisting head into the nearest of those dingy crypts.

It looked like the rest, rusty chain and all. He hardly glanced at the chain. It was the rock that held his bugged-out stare, the dull ginger rock from which these cubicles had been hewn.

He had previously imagined these caves to have been the habitat or ceremonial chambers of some prehistoric tribe long gone and forgotten. But now, with Jones' talk banging through his mind, he was vibrantly aware of pale greenish veins he had not noticed before in the stone which had been left to form the cell partitions. The same greenish tinge O'Toole had marked in that ore!

His daunsy fears abruptly lost in the rush of this new excitement, Medders put the gun away and got the miner's hammer out of his pants and struck the partition a ringing blow. Then, head bent to get the lamp up close, he considered the place with burning eyes; and with pounding heart spun around, breathing hard, to crash his hammer against the ungiving rock that formed the passage's end. Again, and furiously again, he struck that cinnamon wall, finally stepping back to peer exultantly at the flaked-off lines which now disclosed a hidden door.

A rock slab it was, smoothly fitted without handle or knob, adamant as steel against the maul of his hammer, counterbalanced probably to swing on some concealed pivot could a man but find the release that triggered it.

Soaked with sweat, breathing hard, Charlie traced the cracks with trembling fingers, finding no give to the thing at all. Without he could locate the mechanical

122

impulse – the something to be pushed or pulled or whatever – he might have to use dynamite. He could not believe this snug fit had been managed and then caulked with caliche and brushed with mud just to hide a few pots.

"More to it than that," he was telling himself when the lamp on his cap began to splutter.

He grabbed it off and furiously shook it. The light, brightening briefly, commenced despite his best efforts to grow steadily dimmer. Swearing, he dug out his candle, breaking three matches before the wick fired. His sweat turned cold as the monstrous black like some fungoid fog, edging balefully nearer, reduced his vision to the lonely isolation of the candle's feeble flame.

Drawing back uneasily into the angle of the wall, Charlie nervously considered going up for more carbide and maybe bringing down a couple of sticks of Number 1. But as his dubious glance swung once more to assess the stubborn look of this rock the short hairs rose on his neck like hackles. The two vertical cracks exposed by his hammer seemed ... *Yes!*

The slab was moving!

Every muscle congealed in the nightmare grip of horrid fascination immobilizing him,

Medders breathlessly watched the great stone slowly, ponderously, revolve on its axis with no more sound than tumblers dropping behind the gray iron of Jones' Tucson safe. Though his eyes felt about to roll off his cheekbones, Charlie could not have lifted so much as one finger had the Devil himself suddenly stepped from the hole.

Nothing squeezed past the stopped slab of that door; but some things you don't *have* to see to be scared of. Sometimes the things a man knows least about tend to frighten him most.

Nothing came out but a rush of bad air smelling strongly of death – strong enough to move Medders. He was in such a hurry to get out of its touch he went ten flying strides through that boot-banging clamor in his dash for the ladders before discovering his candle had got blown out. He couldn't see a thing. He couldn't stop, either. Terror closed in and, in that suffocating black, he lost all sense of direction, crashing headlong into unyielding rock.

It must have shaken a little sense into him. At least, when he got back enough strength to move, he stayed where he was, ears stretched, heart pounding, for what seemed an eternity. He didn't know what might come out of this murk, but when nothing did he twisted onto all fours and eventually got up. Even then he waited, scarcely daring to draw breath, until his jittery stare found a vague area of grayness which he reckoned to be the shaft.

And it was.

Weak with relief his hands found the ladder. Rung by rung he pulled himself up, wondering if each new hold might not be his last. But when he stepped off at the number 2 level, with nothing untoward having provided further alarm, he was inclined somewhat testily to believe he had let his imagination run away with him, that he'd probably someway triggered that slab himself. He decided, just the same, to stay topside a while until the stink in that passage had had a chance to air out.

Dragging his weight up the final climb it came over him this would be as good a time as any to go bury a few more tins of good water. He was still thinking about it when his head came above the well shaft coping and saw, in the refracted light from the cave's concealed entrance, the closed door to the cabin which he himself had left open.

Still clamped to the ladder in the shock of this discovery, something cold and round came hard against the back of his neck.

XIV

Students of medicine might be surprised to learn how many separate and individual notions – mostly irrelevant – pass through a man's head in moments of crisis while the mind is first staggered by premonitions of disaster.

There was nothing really complicated about Charlie Medders; as a product of his environment he was a pretty average guy. Out of his element, beyond his depth, he had – down below – been up against dreads he could not understand, allowing primitive fears to stampede and make a fool of him.

But a gun dug into the back of his neck was within the realm of familiar experience. He stayed "put" as the saying goes, his strongest emotion one of bitter disgust. "You don't hev to shoot," he growled. "I know when I'm beat."

"All who believe that can stand on their heads! Now, be careful. I'm jumpety as a pocketful of crickets," the voice of Belita Storn remarked dryly, "and you know what they say about excitable women."

Medders, beneath his breath, cursed. It burnt a feller up enough having *anyone* get the drop on him, but to discover he'd let a woman and of all women this one, was a cross no man had ought to have to bear. Still, he wasn't too astonished. With his kind of luck it had been about time for her to throw some more wrenches. He'd been suspecting for some while she might find her way back. "You come by yourself?"

Behind the resentful bitterness of it this sounded like a chump about to pitch in his hand.

But she hadn't come out here to sympathize with him. "Burks and his red brothers are out there someplace – I got a look at them yesterday, off west of Gu Chuapo. You don't have to worry," she advised with a sniff, "they won't show up heve through any carelessness of mine. You can climb out and turn around. But watch yourself, hombre."

Medders looked as disgruntled and fed up as he'd sounded.

This could go either way. She was aware of it and worried, not knowing quite how to say what she had in mind. These burro men were a stiff-necked lot, touchy as teased snakes, and prone to get their backs up over things less notionable persons might not waste a second thought on.

Not finding any better way, she said straight-out: "You ought to have a keeper!"

Medders, beginning to bridle, broke off to peer more carefully at her. "What's that supposed t' mean?"

"You've really fixed yourself up fine, prancing around with that Imogene Winters! You think she'd look twice at a nump like you?"

"Now, just a dang minute –"

"You listen to me! When they were talking it up, didn't you claim any common stock put out for this mine would be nothing but bait to fleece widows and orphans? Yes or no?"

"Sure, but –"

"Then it's not only Jones that's made you look like a panhandling bum! Another meeting was called just before I left town and your prissy friend Winters, all smiles and dimples, sat in with those shares and voted, with T.K. and Heintzleman, to okay that stock." Belita's eyes flashed with scorn. "What will those widows and orphans think now with your picture, big as life, printed right on the face of it!"

Charlie peered at her, stunned. "B-B-But –"

Glaring, she said angrily: "You had
128

Rawlins convinced; even Ferris was worried. When Jones handed around the shares and gave Winters ten signed over by you, I naturally assumed...." She looked at him sharply. "It was Winters' votes –"

"But I only give her *one!*" Medders wailed. Then his cheeks turned hot as he realized how the curvaceous Ginnie had tricked him, substituting ten for the one he had granted her.

"Well," Belita said, having read his face and added a few notions of her own to the total, "I suppose you agreed to trade her a share in return for...umm...value received. You men are such –"

"It wasn't...I was tryin' t' find out," Charlie growled, red to the ears, "what went on after I left. She offered t' show me her notes of the minutes if...."

Belita Storn sniffed. "I'll bet!" The way she snapped out the words made it pretty apparent she reckoned this was not all Ginnie had offered.

Made Charlie feel like a lyin' hound, a dang egg-suckin' skunk, until he happened to remember it was *her* that had brought Jones into this deal. This didn't much help because he knew he looked guilty with his face feeling hotter than a two-dollar pistol; and he began to swell up, too riled to think straight, about ready, by grab, to let her have both barrels. But she abruptly took the wind from his sails, coming right out with what he was fixing to get said.

"You'll be thinking," she smiled, "I haven't much room to talk, turning half of those shares you gave *me* over to Jones – and you're probably right. It was a breach of trust, although I thought at the time...." She shook her head. "No matter. It was a poor thing to do. I can see that, now. With the shares *she* dug out of you, the ones Jones has and the block he grabbed for those bad debts, you're just about back to where you were before –"

"Not quite," Medders growled. "I'm still squattin' on this ore an' – without you've told me – they don't even know where t' start lookin'."

Belita shook her head again. "I haven't told," she said, "but it looks like I'm responsible for most of your hard luck." She reached into her blouse. "Would it help if I gave back –"

"I'm not *that* hard up," Charlie said like he was affronted. "You own half of everything that comes outa here. When I give a person somethin' I *give* it to him – see? An' I don't recognize no company set up by Jones t' milk no bunch of suckers

130

outa what it's taken 'em a lifetime t' save!"

"But that company is legal. You can't –"

"The hell I can't!" Medders said, skinning the lips off his teeth like a sure enough wolf. He peered at her fiercely. "Long's I've got ol' Betsy an' shells t' cram into her there better not nobody come monkeyin' round here!"

In the glitter of that stare Belita kind of shivered. She said dubiously, "I'm not sure...." and appeared to have tied into some stubborn notions of her own. "It's all so mixed up! This *is* the Weeping Widow, you know." She sighed. "You've done a lot for me and it's been hard to live with, knowing how ungrateful I must seem, selling half of what you gave me to that awful banker – and what you just now said about us still being partners, it...it shames me even more."

She dropped her eyes and Medders shuffled his feet. "Well, hell," he gruffed, uncomfortably embarrassed, "you had your reasons, I reckon."

"I – *yes!* I resented you terribly. It was a horrible jolt to find someone here, to have come all the way from Durango only to discover some ignorant desert rat had beaten me to it. I...I saw your burros," she said as though this cleared up everything. But Medders still had his mouth open. She said, color piling into her cheeks: "It was a pretty sneaky thing I did, pretending to be lost and letting you find me ... acting like I was out of my head."

Charlie shrugged. She looked so tore up and humble he told her magnanimously, "No skin lost. Comin' right down t' cases I ain't so lily white myself if it comes t' that."

She stared at him oddly. Perhaps she found it hard to believe a grown man could be such a chump. Recall of other things he had done apparently relieved whatever fleeting disquiet had given her pause. She plunged into her story.

Her mother had been a great Spanish beauty, daughter of an old and socially prominent family which had been living for years on inherited wealth. Belita's father, a transplanted American of considerable dash and charm, one gathered was believed to have been in the Santa Fe trade, though she was frank to admit certain jealous competitiors had spread unproved rumors connecting his wagons with the transport of contraband.

After the death of her mother in a hunting accident, Belita, aged five, had been taken by the Spanish grandparents to raise. She had seen her father but infrequently after this. He had been killed two years later in a quarrel over cards. Fate's bony hand, when she was twelve, had struck again. Cholera swept the city, taking both grandparents. When the courts and the lawyers had finished with their bickerings, and gotten rid of the creditors, the estate had been reduced to a few hundred dollars and a folio of musty time-yellowed papers.

Belita, at fourteen, had been forced to find work. "And what could I do?" she demanded graphically of Medders. "I had been trained in graces befitting a station I could no longer claim." There'd been no other relatives she could go to. When the money ran out there had seemed but two choices, the streets or the convent. Desperate, she had finally persuaded Gregorio Guttierez, a tavern keeper, to let her sing in his bar for room and board. "It was terrible!" she cried, regarding Medders slanchways through the curl of sorrel lashes. "You've no idea what that place was like," she said with a visible shudder.

Charlie's face should have been a great comfort. He looked as though he had lived every minute of it.

And then one night about two months ago, unable to put up with any more of it, she said, she had fled the place in the gypsy clothes she'd had to don for her "appearances" and a handful of pesos she had taken from the till.

Among the musty papers she'd received from the grandparents' estate was a map she had cherished, and this had given her the strength to break away from Guttierez. She'd made up her mind to come to Arizona and find the wonderful mine her great-grandfather had been forced to abandon during the Indian revolt of 1751.

She hadn't had too much trouble getting out of Durango, but had been turned back at the border by the immigration authorities. With sixteen summers she had become a desirable woman able to pass herself off as a gitana of the Bear Folki and so found work as a flamenco dancer among the dives of Juarez and Agua Prieta where one night she had crossed the border with smugglers.

Medders was regarding her with something close to awe. As she paused for breath, he said, shaking his head: "I can't see how you ever done it – all them miles! Just a chit of a girl –"

"A girl, when she has to, can do many things. I was desperate, you understand. Something in here" – she clapped a hand to her breast – "something deep inside was driving me. Where there is a will God will show the way. Without His help, and the intercession of the Saints, I would never have got here."

"An' the map," Medders said. "Hows about my havin' a squint at it?"

"Of course," Belita smiled and, reaching inside the neck of her mannish new shield-fronted shirt, passed over a square of folded paper.

Charlie's face was a study. But as he smoothed it against the shaft coping, disbelief and astonishment were swiftly replaced by a lively interest. This was a map, all right, replete with a set of hand lettered directions. He bent over it, mumbling as he spelled out the words.

Belita, having meanwhile put away her derringer, smiled more widely as he looked up from the paper to meet the challenge of her stare. "Now do you believe?"

But Medders' eyes were narrowed. A frown was twisting the whisker-scraggled cheeks. "If, like you say, this was your great-gran'pappy's mine, how come this stuff – all them directions an' such – ain't written in Spanish? An' if it was that long ago when he skipped out how come this paper ain't fell plumb apart?"

135

The girl laughed. "Because it's new paper, silly; a copy I made myself."

Charlie tapped the map with a knobby finger. "It don't say Weepin' Widder, it says Esmeralda."

"My grandmother had a bracelet set with pieces of ore taken out of this mine. Many times I have seen it. The ore is the same. This is the place or I could not have come here. The mountains, the buttes, every landmark is here. My people named it Esmeralda for the color of the ore. How must one have to convince you, hombre? Look –" she said, and touched the map. "C-A-V-E spells *cave*, does it not?"

Medders grudgingly nodded. Then he said like it hurt him: "I reckon it's yours."

XV

"Ours," she corrected, pumping his hand. "We're partners – remember? Full partners," she grinned, nodding with approval as Charlie's look perked up. "It was the gringos, new people coming in after your General Kearny took New Mexico away from us, that gave this Weeping Widow tag

136

to it. Perhaps we should call it Esmeralda like great-grandfather –"

"Changing the name won't stand in Jones' way."

"Back in Durango I have the original Perez map. . . ."

"The courts wouldn't recognize a claim based on that. It's been a lost mine for more'n a hundred years, an' the law around here eats right outa that polecat's paw. Nope," Medders scowled, "we'll have t' keep her hid an' sell off the ore in dribbles an' drabs."

She looked at him doubtfully.

"There ain't no other way," he growled. "That highbinder's got his foot in now an' with them shares an' that company. . . ." He threw up his hands. "You oughta know by now how that bustard operates. He'd skin a flea fer its hide an' taller!"

She looked a little let down. "I guess there's not much chance of selling ore in Tucson. What did you get for that load you brought in?"

"Under five thousan', time I got done with it," Medders growled, remembering. "An' then got beat outa most of that! But there's other places." His face wrinkled up as he thought about some. "Be a heap longer haul," he told her at last, "an' we'd hev t' watch out fer Burks an' them Injuns, but if we could git it to a stampmill we'd be paid what it's worth."

He passed back her map, braced a hip against the coping. "First I'll have t' set up some more springs – it can git pretty dry chasin' around in that desert." He recollected something else but before he could get it shaped into words she cut in to ask: "If we had more burros couldn't we take out more?"

"You got someone in mind wants t' give away a dozen?"

"No, but –"

"I been thinkin', he said, gruffer still with his tone. "Jones threatened t' hev me in court over you – somethin' about chain marks an' keepin' you pris'ner. You tell him that?"

It was her eyes that dropped. Looking pretty uncomfortable, she faced him straightly. "I said you kept me chained like a peon – I had to tell him *something!* I thought, being a banker, he would have enough money to open this mine...."

Medders stared at her, scowling. She saw his fists clench. She backed off a little, eyes widening, wary. "An' the marks?" Medders said.

She gnawed at her lip. Finally, sighing, she
138

slipped off a boot and shyly poked the foot toward him. "They're about gone now."

They were, for a fact. But the scars could be seen, pale ridges of tissue, suggestive and ugly. Charlie wasn't looking too pleasant himself. "What made 'em?"

"Well...if you must know, I did." Rather plaintively she added, "I had to have something to back up my story...."

"Yeah. Like that bracelet," Medders said, "an' the map you fixed up. What did T.K. think of it?"

She drew back with a gasp. Color rushed into stiffened cheeks through which her stare burned like fanned coals. Slowly brightness faded. "I guess I had that coming," she said, but stood her ground, almost pleading now. "You can't really think I'd do a thing like that?"

Looking bitterly again at the signs of her duplicity Medders blew through his teeth but grudgingly shook his head. Jones, if he'd ever got a squint at that map, would have had his understrappers around here thicker than cloves on a Christmas ham. But she'd have seen that, too! Eyes sharp as hers wasn't like to.... "Ahr," he said, "t' hell with it!"

But she caught his arm as he was about to stride off. "Can't you see I'm trying to be *honest* with you?"

139

"While you're bein' so honest why'd you come back? Afraid I'd make off with what was left of this stuff?"

"That's a brutal thing to say to a friend who threw up a sure thing to come out here and help you –"

"All who believe that can go stand on their heads," Medders mimicked, disgusted. Face darkening, he said, "It's friends like you a guy had better watch out fer!" and, flinging off her hand, went stomping into the cabin.

When he came out with the Sharps she was just where he'd quit her, an arrested shape against the shaft coping. "You're... going?" There was no hope left in that voice.

"That's right – put the blame on *me!*" Charlie growled, but she didn't lash back as he'd expected her to. She seemed someway sort of lost and defenseless and, though he wouldn't have put it that way, more appealing. Her sorrel mane, pulled back in the Spanish fashion, gave her the look of a skinned rabbit. "I'm not in a position to blame anyone," she said in a very small voice.

This was certainly news. He stared at her, puzzled.

Her eyes looked oddly soft and swimmy. "If you would only change your mind...."

140

She said abruptly: "Here – you keep the map, hostage to my continued good faith. It may help you believe I've been telling the truth...I really *did* come back to make amends if I could."

He would sooner have looked to find a bull in bloomers than to hear her talking like the meek were about to do their inheriting and there could still be hope she'd find her name in the pot. She had something up her sleeve and you could lay to that!

"All right," she said with a shaky little laugh. "I suppose in your eyes I'm a first class Judas goat, a conniving Jezebel, a Delilah of the wastelands. I guess, in your place, I might be suspicious too. But I'd never walk off without giving you a chance."

Medders, who hadn't the least intention of stepping out of this, grunted. He'd picked up the rifle, thinking to have a look around. "Where-at was they working' when them Injuns run 'em off?"

She said reluctantly, "I don't know."

"Didn't figure you did. Well," he said, tearing up her map until it looked like something the rats had been at, "we got mebbe a week – ten days if we're lucky, before your Tucson banker friend gits around t' really bearin' down.

She was watching as though she couldn't quite believe it the tiny bits of paper fluttering away from his fists. He said, grinning sourly, "So we'll hev to' move fast." And, when her stare came up, he handed her his cap. "You'll find carbide fer this inside the shack. I'll be away fer a bit. If you're minded t' do somethin' helpful, see if you can uncover that ore face – an' keep outa sight. Bushwhacker bullets don't care who they smack."

It took the best part of two nights and a tagalong day to get his water buried where, should this deal turn sticky, it might make the precious difference between what would suit Jones and what he'd settle for himself.

Watching the sun drop over the hump and begin its long slide toward the darker side of things, Charlie was reminded that his petticoat partner might be having to make do on some pretty slim pickings back there at the mine with that horror he'd uncovered.

He was anxious to get back, but Begetta was tough and with a bit of pushing could probably raise Tubac inside three-four hours. Tubac, oldest town founded by white men in the territory and seat of the first newspaper – the *Weekly Arizonian* – was now, owing to the spasmodic attentions of hostile Apaches, in a pretty advanced state of decay. But a handful of families, most of them Mexican, still eked out a living from peaches, pomegranates and a few hills of maize, and a general store had managed to keep open in the interest of roundabout ranches.

The girl and himself would need more grub, and those twenty-five loaded shells for the Sharps might go pretty fast if Jones decided to really clamp down. Food and cartridges were prime necessities; he still had what cash he'd picked up from that Tucson hotel room. He decided to risk it.

Lavender shadows lay long across the range and, by the look and smells, Tubac was sitting down to supper when Charlie and Begetta trudged wearily past the white-plastered adobe Roman Catholic church. He left Begetta at the livery happily munching oats, and walked around to the store where the first thing he purchased was four boxes of cartridges, one for his pistol and the rest for the Sharps. Then he ordered up two sacks of flour, salt, sow belly and fifty pounds of beans, reluctantly deciding not to weight himself down with tinned stuffs. Then he made a quick supper on a can of tomatoes, a slab of cheese and some crackers, paid his bill, ran a hand through his whiskers and said he'd be back.

There was a guy in the chair when he stepped through the barber's door, and another gent reading the hair tonic labels from a bench by the door while he waited. "Just getting my ears freed," this one said with a grin as Medders started to back off. "Say!" The man's eyes suddenly sharpened. "Aren't you Charlie Medders, the feller that opened –"

But Medders was already out in the street. Heating his axles he took off round a corner, ducked into a passage between empty store fronts, came out breathing hard and made a bee line for the livery, blessedly in sight less than half a block away.

Short of reaching it, really puffing now, a rabbity look twisted over his shoulder having glimpsed no commotion, he dropped into a walk. He couldn't recollect ever seeing the guy before, but he'd been given a fright and wasn't over it yet. Jones had a mighty long arm in this country, and plenty of jaspers not on his paysheet was sure not above trying to curry his favor.

Still panting and glowering, Charlie, all nerves, swung into the runway, discovering the proprietor, perched on a crate, leisurely shaving a stick.

144

"Didn't take you long t' go through our town."

Medders peered at him suspiciously but let the thought go. "You got three mules in that corral out there. What's the rock bottom price on them?"

The stableman scrinched up his eyes for a look. "Hundred apiece on them two browns. That there sand-colored jigger ort t' bring about fifty." He considered Charlie cagily. "Make it three twenty-five fer the lot and they're yours."

Charlie scowled toward the backs of those two empty buildings. "Throw in a saddle," he grumbled, "an' it's a deal."

The proprietor, briefly hesitating, decided not to push his luck. "Done!" he declared; and was getting up to go find a kak for this gullible pilgrim when Charlie, bent under the pull of a leadshank, came dragging Begetta away from the feed rack. "Git 'em ready t' travel, an' lash on a couple sacks of cracked oats," he called. "I'll be back directly."

With Begetta snubbed to a porch post he went into the store and hurried out with his provisions, including as an afterthought a gray flannel shirt and a pair of Texas pants for Belita. It was while he was tieing these purchases in place that a voice spoke up so

145

close to his elbow he pretty near jumped clean over Begetta.

Full dark had by this time closed down the view, but in the light shafting out of the storekeeper's windows Charlie found himself confronted by the one man in town he had hoped to avoid, the derby-hatted jasper who had accosted him at the barber's.

"Name is Jennison Jelks," the guy said, boring in, "local correspondent for the Arizona *Republic* – all I want is to get something authentic on this whopping development your company's issuing stock for." He was talking fast with his ingratiating grin, trying to keep Medders pinned till he could get enough out of him to send to his paper. "Hell, you're a hero! A single-blanket jackass prospector who, with nothing but persistence and his own ingenuity, has apparently uncovered the biggest find of the century. Is it really as big as – Here, wait! Have a heart...."

Medders, who had been fidgeting to get away, relaxed enough from his fright to grumble, scowling suspiciously: "What do you want me to say?"

"Just give us the truth. Something I can tell fifty-four hundred readers bustin' to get their teeth into notions that haven't stemmed mainly from a desire to sell stock."

"All right," Charlie said, beginning to take a grim pleasure from this. "I don't know what's comin' out Company headquarters, but I can state for a fact there ain't been a lick of development done in that mine since I opened it up."

The reporter stared skeptically. "According to the prospectus –"

"That come straight outa the mouth of T.K. Jones!"

"I can't print that," Jelks said, disgusted.

"Why not? You asked fer the truth an', by grab, you're gittin' it. The whole thing's a fraud. All that's back of that stock is a bunch of hot air, an' you can say I said so."

Jelks, with a notebook propped against his belly, was writing like mad. "I can quote you on that?"

"Word fer word," Charlie growled. "An' you can furthermore say I told you flat out the whole deal smells so bad I give up my seat on the Board, refused any share in the Company an' washed my hands of the whole swindlin' works. You can tell your readers I'm thinkin' of suing them buggers for defamation of character in the unauthorized use of my picture on them certificates."

Jelks scribbled this down, then looked up to peer at Medders rather queerly for a moment. "But it was my understanding you

147

fetched in several sacks of this ore... Mr. Jones –"

"Yeah! He says a heap of things besides his prayers! He's the topdog crook of the whole shebang!"

The reporter, shifting his stance, eyed Medders uneasily. "That's a pretty wild accusation, you know, against a man as big as Tiberius Jones." He chewed on his pencil, torn between doubt and the burning desire to make the most of what this fool had been giving him. Caution finally got the best of him.

Medders could see that. "Listen!" he growled, and proceeded to blurt out the whole story of Jones' connection with the Weeping Widow, including a description of the various squeeze plays put on by the banker to take over the company and load the market with stock that was strictly pie in the sky. "Them certificates ain't worth a quarter of what you'd git fer a trunkful of Confederate shinplasters! Don't take my word fer it," he said; "ask the girl!"

Jelks looked dubious. He seemed sympathetic but distrustful when he said, "You might be telling me the gospel truth but I'm afraid it's no go. The only way my paper would go to press with that story would be over your name. Too bad, but there it is."

Charlie, with one of his twisted grins, took the stub of pencil and blackly wrote his name across the bottom of Jelks' notes. "An' while you're at it," he said, "it might pay off fer you to spend a mite of time in the recorder's office. Then ask that great hypothecator just where this wonderful mine is at."

Having said which, he untied Begetta from her mooring at the porch and went off through the dark to pick up his three mules.

XVI

During the hours he spent getting back to the mine Charlie not infrequently astonished his mules with the guffaws and belly laughs that came jouncing out of him from picturing Jones' face when that story got around. The tycoon of Tucson would sure have his hands full keeping up his front bombarded by the questions and letters pouring in with demands for an accounting!

Not all of those miles were covered in such glee. He had some conscience stricken intervals when he thought about Belita coming onto that chamberful of dried-up wretches left to starve to death behind the

149

rock door. At the time he had figured it would serve her right and that she'd sure had it coming, but there was moments when he felt pretty meaching about her, stuck off there alone with such ghastly reminders of her family's shame.

More often, however, and with increasing disquiet, he got to worrying about himself and the hereafter looming larger every time he poked a squint at it. It came over him maybe he had been a mite hasty pricking the bubble of this stock fraud, and all, the way he had. Jones, when he got enough over that punch to catch a fresh breath, would be several shades closer to full-scale explosion than a case of thawed dynamite left to dry by an open fire.

Humiliated, publicly embarrassed and denied the loot his machinations had been aimed at, he would be not only cram-jammed with fury but brought to realize his only chance of recapturing his former high place in the community was to prove possession of a mine he didn't have – and not even this would be really sufficient. He would certainly have to produce a bonanza or, skewered by Medders' exposure, get out of the country. And it did not take much figuring to understand which he was most likely to try for.

Clutched with the nag of these nerve-frazzling glimpses Charlie lost several hours profanely endeavoring to louse up his trail. He plowed through sand he might otherwise have skirted; at one stretch he spent upwards of ninety minutes working his animals through a maze of broken rock ledges and then, still pursued by visions of his come-uppance, cut over into Papago country west of the Baboquivaris where he frittered away another half day trying to buy additional mules and engage a crew with nothing more substantial to put into the deal than promises.

These heroic efforts resulted in seven sorry-looking long-eared specimens blown up in the bargaining to three times their worth and five teen-age boys – obvious malcontents – whose worth was untried and so plainly debatable no one less desperate than Medders would have even looked twice at them.

What he had wanted were several case-hardened bucks who would do what he told them and not cloud the issue with a lot of fool questions. But time was running out on him; he took what he could get and hung onto his temper.

He now had quite a caravan to string out over these empty miles, and the size of it did not noticeably lighten the burden of his thoughts. On the contrary, he grew steadily more concerned about the diminished chances of eluding discovery. So much so that he put two of his schoolboys behind the last mule with branches of mesquite and vigorous orders to wipe out all signs of their passage.

The self elected segundo of this bunch was a pock-faced delinquent with an oversized nose and two mismatched eyes who went, he said, by the name of Heap Walker, and who apparently found very little in life which could approach the satisfaction he got from his own voice. He carried an old and beat-up Henry repeater and was, he told Medders, the world's greatest marksman.

It was the middle of the following day, and hotter than the hinges of hell's hip pocket, when Charlie finally sighted the hills that hid the Weeping Widow. Impatient as he was, he did not swing directly toward them but antigodled around to come up from the south behind an outlying spur which concealed the secret trail he had worked out through the rocks. He had no more than put the dun mule into an apparent slant for this than the pock-nosed Walker, breaking into a torrent of hard sounding Papago, came whittle-whanging up with a look black as thunder.

152

"No go there! Bad place, them hill!"

Charlie hooked a knee around his hull's cracked horn. "Yeah? What's the matter with it?"

Walker, waving his arms, cried excitedly: "Bad place! Heap bad!" and the rest of the Papagos, long faced and edgy, looked about ready to dig for the tules.

Medders said, scowling, "What the hell have I got here, a bunch of damn squaws?"

Walker's look turned darker. His stringy arms were folded across his greasy white man's vest. When he failed to stare Medders down the Papago stuck out a dirty claw. "Injun go home. Pay now."

Charlie didn't know what had got into their craws but he had put too much sweat and worry into this to sit calmly by while an ignorant savage kicked the props out from under him. Lifting the Sharps off his lap he said with its bore fixed on Walker's chest: "You hired out t' do a piece of work. Now git up there an' do it."

The fellow skinned back his lips in a horrible grimace and showed the whites of his eyes but in the end, very ugly, jerked his mount's head around and kicked it on up the trail, the rest of the crew sullenly filing past to fall in behind.

Sleeving sweat off his cheeks and

apprehensively wondering what Belita would be making of this, he gave the burro a nod and, rounding up the loose mules, went nervously clattering after them. From up there she'd not be able to see who they were, not anyways to pick out faces. About all he needed right now was to have her open up with that pocket gun!

But nothing untoward occurred. His schoolboys were waiting in a shivery huddle when he rounded the last rock and came in sight of the cave. He motioned them off toward the hay trap. "Turn these critters in there. When you git back we'll stir up some grub."

He was a lot more worried than he saw fit to let on. Considering what was down below he'd expected the girl to be camped up here, and finding no sign of her scared the bejazus out of him.

Of course she may have skedaddled, he reminded himself with a queer, unexpected feeling of emptiness, but even as the notion tramped through his head it seemed a lot less than likely. She had shown too much grit, too much brass bound gall, to let any bunch of dead Injuns run her off. *But what if that trick door had shut on her?*

His stomach turned over and crawled at the thought. Cold sweat cracked through the pores of his skin and his knees got to shaking before common sense caught a strong enough grip to shove back this horror and show it up for sheer nonsense. No girl would walk into a hole filled with mummies.

Someway he was not much comforted. Saying so didn't make it so. Not many girls would, but Belita might. She had enough guts to charge hell with a bucket, and the last thing he'd told her. . . . The shakes came back as he remembered his words. *If you're minded t' do somethin' helpful, see if you can uncover that ore face.*

Of course she'd gone in! He could see her standing there, realizing her debt to him, squaring her jaw. She'd have conquered her revulsion, the things that had driven Charlie back himself – this was the test, the chance she had pleaded for . . . her opportunity to prove herself a pardner he could depend on. *She was in there now.* He could see that rock door, like some carnivorous plant, slowly, stealthily closing behind her.

With a snarling curse Medders tore through the curtain of breaking brush, scrambled into the cave and – in that moment of blindness while his vision adjusted – strode headlong into something roundly rigid that sent the breath whistling through his teeth.

155

There is something about the snout of a firearm that is seldom mistaken for anything else. Stopped cold in his tracks there wasn't much Medders could do but goggle and try to suck in his gut. Even the return of his sight was no great advantage in the glare of those eyes blazing into his own.

"I –"

"Don't open your mouth!" Belita Storn said in a voice that would have broke off a white oak post. For moments they stood like things backed out of wood in a stillness rasped only by the jerk of her breathing. In a flutter of sound leaching in from outside he could feel the shake of her hand through the gun steel.

Then, abruptly, she pulled the pistol away and stepped back.

Charlie stayed where he was. She said, "I can't do it!" and whirled in a swirl of skirts and stalked off.

Not till then did Medders draw a full-grown breath, and mighty near came apart with it. Only the barefooted slap of hurrying feet going past galvanized him enough to take him stumbling through brush to fling a tremulous shout at his departing hired hands.

XVII

Charlie sighed like he had the whole world on his back.

He did have some problems. They were beginning to close in like the Sioux on Custer, but one thing stood out too plain to miss. Let these boys get away from him and he could sure wave goodbye to any chance of getting out the rest of that ore.

He could see that creepy Heap Walker's black stare and the magpie looks of at least a couple others twisting round to take his measure. To get respect from their kind you had to show you could command it.

He raised the Sharps. This could prove kind of tricky what with all them rocks, the drop and desperate energy put into their flight by the lift of that rifle. He pushed the aperture of the sight vane up to the 200-yard mark, squinted carefully, picked a finger of rock that leaned out over the trail, found a crotch to rest the barrel on and waited for his quarry to come into the target area.

The loudmouthed Walker, going hellity larrup, was the first to come bounding into the lens. Medders opened his mouth, quit breathing, and squeezed off. The recoil belted his shoulder. The deep-throated boom of exploded powder went whamming out over the canyon's rock faces with the ground shaking racket of a battery of howitzers. Through the rolling white stench the stone finger flew apart in a burst of shattered fragments not three jumps ahead of that high-bounding Walker.

The insurrection was over.

They came dragging themselves back, mean-eyed, sullen but cowed – at least for the moment. Past the white cheeked Belita, Charlie, poker eyed and ready, motioned them into the cave one by one until it came Walker's turn, the last of the lot. He was the only one packing a firearm and Medders curtly told him to give it to Belita.

He broke into a gabble that Charlie cut short. "You won't have any use fer it down below. When it's needed we'll see. Now git out to that hay trap an' fetch them supplies."

"Send boy –"

"I'm sendin' *you!*"

The pock-nosed Papago was not a reassuring sight. Snake-eyed with rage and humiliation, cut up like he was from flying rock, he looked positively poisonous. But that

158

buffalo gun was powerful medicine. With a final snarl he slammed down his rifle and struck off up the trail like a wetfooted cat.

Charlie picked up the Henry, held it out to Belita. Face expressionless as pounded clay, she considered him a moment before taking the repeater; it was Medders' look that twisted free. He said, turning red, "I, ah – fetched you a present."

Something passed through her eyes, gone as quick as smoke. Her mouth tightened up. "It's no good," she said, pushing the hair off her cheek. "You were right all the time ... this deal is played out."

Charlie's face had the look of a new-hatched nestling, a little bit puzzled but confidently waiting for mama to drop the worm. His bewilderment grew when all she did was stand there. "If you mean you're fed up –"

This brought an impatient snort. She said irritably: "Can't you understand! We've *got* all there is! I found what you were looking for – it was behind that door." She shuddered. "They quit in borrasca. There's nothing left to mine."

"Oh...." Medders said, and perceptibly brightened. "Then all we got t' worry about –"

"You sound," she cried sharply, "like you couldn't care less!"

He peered at her, baffled. "Well, it's simpler this way. Takes a load off my mind if you want the plain truth. Alls we got t' do now is pack out what's showin'. One trip an' we're clear." He told about his talk with Jennison Jelks, the Tubac correspondent for the big Phoenix paper. "One's about all we're goin' t' have time fer, an' we better git at it."

She looked at him slanchways, like maybe he'd grown an extra head in the course of this conversation. Her expression was so peculiar Charlie twisted around, half expecting to find Heap Walker sneaking up on him, but nobody was in sight. "Soon as that bugger fetches in the stuff I brought," he said, "mebbe you better stir up a batch of grub. We'll be at this all night an' –"

"I believe you really *enjoy* chasing rainbows!"

When he stared at her blankly she said, "How long have you been stumbling around after burros?"

"Prospectin'? Seven-eight years, give or take a couple months."

"That's what I mean!" She sounded exasperated. "All that time! Living from hand to mouth, spending your life at the tag

160

end of noplace, talking up a storm to some waggle-eared jack – is *that* what you want?"

Medders, hiking his hat to where it fell precariously across one eye, scratched the back of his head while he studied her, baffled, from beneath the flopped brim. "I never was much fer towns...."

She looked even more put out than she had sounded. It was kind of hard to figure with her raking him over like he hadn't the gumption to pound sand down a rat hole. Then he got it, too late. She'd pushed through the manzanita, leaving him with the jumbled whirl of his thoughts, incredulously staring at her disappearing back.

It always had been enough but now – in spite of his distrust – he wasn't sure about anything. When the pock-faced Walker came staggering down from the hay trap with the stuff he'd got off Begetta, Medders waved him on into the cave, scarcely seeing him. He was, by then, neck deep in the engulfing flood her remarks had let loose, kicking out in all directions in the half-strangled hope of somewhere finding a piece of bottom solid enough to let him come to grips with himself.

It just didn't work out. He fell back on habit as he nearly always did when discovering himself out of step with events.

161

It was easier to drift and kind of bend with the pressure of things that looked too fierce to be coped with. Most knotty problems, he had found, would get impatient like that girl and take themselves off if a man had the wit to sit tight and let them.

The cave, when he finally squirmed his way into it, was filled with light coming out of the shack along with the sounds and stomach-stirring smells whipped up by things Belita had on the stove. The irate Walker and his surly schoolboys had their heads together in a huddle by the shaft; he wasn't bothered by that. He didn't give a whack how mutinous they looked long as none of them got their mitts on a gun. They probably all had knives, but there wasn't enough spunk in the whole kit and caboodle to go up against the Sharps if he could just stay awake and keep his eyes skinned.

What did get under his hide was the *feel* of things around here. He could always tell when a storm was building up by the misery of aches that got to pulling on his bones. It had nothing to do with them Injuns. The pressure was coming right out of that shack along with the heat kicked up by the stove.

When he couldn't tolerate this discomfort any longer he took himself over to lounge a while in the open door. Chicken pox and measles was things a waddy couldn't fight, and any guy what valued his peace of mind was bound sooner or later to put women right along with 'em. Like them or not, there was things in this world a feller had to go along with, and red headed women was at the top of the list.

And it got mighty quick plain if there was to be any meeting of minds in this matter Medders was going to have to take the first step. This graveled him, too, for he could tell she figured she had right on her side. "You find that shirt an' them pants –"

She skewered him with a bitter glance, and only then did he notice she had the duds on. It made him feel like a fool. He didn't know what to say, hardly, and put it down in his mind as another mark against her. But he presently scraped up voice enough to say, apropos of the truths that lay festering in him: "I make out well enough, if that was what you meant. I look after my own. 'Tain't so much what I find as the lookin' that pleasures me."

She loosed a kind of sniff, never glancing around. She shoved one pot back, jabbed a spoon in another and stirred with such a clatter even the Papagoes out by the shaft looked up. "Just a flat-footed bum," she

163

remarked with disdain. "I will never marry a man who won't work."

Medders gawped, but the gall of her got the best of him. "I'm not the marryin' kind!" he snarled, and glowered fierce as any bot-bit bull. "No pants-wearin' female will ever git *me* up in front of no preacher!"

She tossed the spoon in the pot. "Come an' get it," she yelled, "before I throw it away."

XVIII

Charlie fumed and fretted his way through the meal, hardly knowing what he put into him, scarcely peering any higher than the freckled and florid perfection of Belita's sleeve-rolled arms. He could have eaten fried curbstone with about as much pleasure.

He had no thought for the chomp and clatter of the voracious schoolboys. Two goals kept top priority through the churn and lash of his seething visions – getting through and getting out. Yet here, once more, he was faced with the girl.

Had it not been so bitterly impossible he'd have played off the rest of this deal plumb solo. But it just wasn't in the cards, and he knew it. Squirm and wriggle as he could and did he was turned back from every strategy by the graveling realization that without Belita's help he was not going to get this ore out in time.

It wasn't in Medders to pull out empty-handed; he wouldn't even consider such a weaselly solution. This was *his* ore; he wasn't about to walk out on it. And yet it wasn't the prospect of gain that held him; he'd gotten by before and could do it again. It was the *principle,* that's what it was...the unpalatable notion of being beat out of it!

He might lack a few jumps of under-standing females, but bankers and the ways of the desert he savvied. Even so, this would be no trip for weak hearts; it could be touch and go every step of the way. He saw this, accepted it. Every facet of the plan had got to mesh and mesh right and it could be no better than what was put into it.

He had to put in what lay ready to hand, the mules he'd picked up, these Papago packers...his own life and...maybe even Belita's. He didn't waste time wondering what he would do if it didn't work out.

He got up and said bluntly: "We're goin' t' move ore, try to pack it t' Charleston, over beyond the Santa Ritas. It ain't goin' t' be easy. We'll probably run into gunfire. But if we git this stuff through, every galoot that's on tap when we deliver it at the T.M. & M. will have a equal share of whatever we git fer it."

He watched them a moment, put up a hand to quell the gabble of voices. "I know. I promised t' pay fer them mules, promised you boys wages, but this way you'd stand t' make a heap more. Them in favor of the original deal put your paws up."

The Papagos looked at each other. Medders could see they weren't happy, but no hands came up. "All right," he said, "it'll be share an' share alike. Now the longer this takes the bigger the chance we'll run into trouble, so let's git at it. You an' you" – he pointed out Walker and the youngest of the bunch, a dark burly hombre who called himself Flores – "will work down below. With me," he smiled grimly. "You," he said, singling out another, "will go fetch in the stock, an' then do whatever the girl here says. There's the winch to be worked, the ore t' be sacked and packed on them critters. Figure t' be movin' afore first light."

He passed a long stare about, watching them through the cracks of his eyes. "One more thing." He let the stillness pile up. "I taken you into this deal as full brothers. I see anythin' don't fit that picture this buff'ler gun won't be waitin' around fer no *re*peat performance. It won't be knockin' no rocks down neither!"

When the sun peered over the rimrocks, slanting its bright fire across the cold sands, Operation Mulepack was well under way.

Belita, on the flop-eared dun colored Eduardo who had fetched her lovely lies into Tucson and more recently brought her penitently back, was well out in front riding point. After her, strung out like a Mexican smuggler caravan over most of a quarter mile, came the heavy-laden mules plodding briskly along to the barks and jabs of the prod-carrying strawhatted Papagos, Charlie Medders on Begetta watchfully bringing up the rear.

Every animal carried a full waterskin in addition to its pack, and Medders carried his big Sharps rifle prominently displayed, but there were no tinkling bells – so beloved by the runners of contraband – to herald their progress. And there was very little talking.

They nooned at a dry lake some ten or twelve miles southwest of the Cerro Colorados and, after resting the mules for an hour, re-packed and pushed on, cutting north of Arivaca across the flanks of the San Louis Mountains where the going, not too

167

bad, offered a little more protection than could be found on the yucca studded flats they'd left behind.

Charlie wasn't too keen about having Belita away off there at the front after that talk he had thrown at the schoolboys. Cutting the pie in seven pieces he didn't reckon would be sitting too well with her – not that he figured it would come to that; but if it did she'd have less than she might have got from Jones. He couldn't help being uneasy about her, but Walker he didn't trust out of his sight.

He'd told her at noon, when he was setting up the route, they'd stop again about five and pull the packs off the mules for a couple hours' rest. He wanted to keep all the strength he could in them against the time when they might have to run. Tomorrow they'd be climbing through some pretty rough country.

At about four-thirty, by the look of his shadow, Charlie rode Begetta into the gut of a draw and found Belita, above a fire of dead mesquite fronds, already working with the food for their supper while the Papagos were still hauling packs off the mules. Looking the animals over he came back and told Walker to hang onto the oats and put the critters out on hobbles. "We'll

168

be layin' over here till the moon comes up."

Which was about two hours longer than he'd figured to be here, but on what they could forage they would need that much rest. Belita, too, seemed kind of gray in the face.

He could have used some shuteye himself if it wasn't for feeling he had to keep his eyes peeled. So far everything had gone like clockwork, but Walker's good behavior wasn't fooling him at all.

Soon as the grub was cooked Medders stomped out the fire, and after they had eaten he climbed a rocky point and stared out over the darkening landscape, finding nothing to alarm him though he watched for half an hour. Restless and edgy he came lugging his worries back into camp to find Flores industriously sharpening a knife, the rest lolling around like they was too full to poop. Then Charlie, counting noses, came up one short. Pock faced big-nosed Walker was missing!

With a curse Medders whirled to look for Belita. Already afoot and moving toward him, she called: "What's wrong?"

The night had thickened to where you couldn't much more than make out faces, but he could tell by her voice she was edgy as he was. Sight of Walker's rifle in her hands took some of the teeth from the sharpest of his worries. He spun away without answering, running toward the mules, slowing as he saw their heads come up, stopping when one of them snorted.

He heard the girl stop behind him while his eyes combed the shadows, heard the mule grunt again. "Walker!"

The guttural bark of a laugh fell out of the murk. A deeper blackness took shape and moving nearer became unmistakably the man he was seeking. "W'at you want?"

"Thought you might be gittin' ready to slope."

"You nervous, Boss? Me check mule." The Papago grinned.

"Back up," Medders growled, "I want a look at that critter."

It was wasted breath. There was nothing to see when Walker pointed him out. Medders felt the mule over, could find nothing wrong beyond the obvious fact the pockmarked segundo had got back his cockiness. Charlie, grinding his teeth, waved the man back to camp. "What is it?" Belita whispered as they fell in behind.

"I dunno," Medders grunted, stare fixed on that shuffling shape. "He never come out here t' scratch his butt. You watch out fer that jigger. He's slipperier'n slobbers."

The ugly Papago was tickled over something, and such high spirits were plumb unlikely in a buck who had lost as much face as Heap Walker. If he'd lamed any of the mules....

Back in camp, still fuming, Charlie peered around suspiciously. The rest of the redskins were sprawled like dropped logs, hats over faces, a couple of them filling the night with raucous snores. Medders, suddenly stiffening, loosed a furious shout. "All right, you possum-playin' coyotes! Git me some light!" he snarled at Belita.

Another boy was missing – he'd looked twice, recounting heads, to make sure. As the fire blazed up he discovered it was the youngest, the burly youth called Flores.

He looked minded to take Heap Walker by the throat. "Where is he?"

Black eyes stared sullenly. "Boy 'fraid, I guess," Walker said. "Go home."

Charlie struggled with his rage, knowing he could not afford any more mistakes. "What'd he have t' be scairt of?"

"No like go down that hole. Heap bad," Walker grumbled. "Cave of dead. Mebbeso spirit –"

"Don't pigeon-talk me, you sorghum faced reprobate – you can do better'n that!"

The pock-nosed Walker with an elaborate
171

shrug mumbled something in Papago about "lost spirits" and "Ancient Ones" and, folding his arms, relapsed into silence.

Medders knew enough about those Ancient Ones – the people who had been on this land before the Papagos – to know this educated schoolboy was giving him the runaround. But, short of working him over Apache-style, and he didn't for a minute reckon the girl would stand for that, there wasn't no way he could dig the truth out of them. He had an uneasy feeling juning around through his system that Flores' departure was hooked up to this ore.

"Mistake I made," he said, eyeing them bitterly, "was tryin' t' treat Injuns like they was halfway human, but don't count on me makin' the same mistake twice." He got four shells for the Sharps out of a pocket and held them up where the light could strike across them. "I'm goin' t' read you what it says on the noses of these buggers: Ramon, Jacinto, Ricardo, Walker – one of 'em fer each of you. Next boy that wanders off is goin' t' git lost an' *stay* lost. Now pack them mules, we're gittin' outa here pronto!"

They made three brief stops during the night to rest the animals, some ninety minutes all told, Charlie stomping around with his

Sharps and his cursing, begrudging every instant they were not upon the trail. And there was more to his desire to cover ground than baseless fright. Two discoveries had been made which increased the florid complexion of Flores' disappearance. Belita's pocket pistol had sprouted wings and her faithful steed, the angular flop-eared Eduardo, had turned up missing while the mules were being packed. This was all Medders needed to clinch his conviction the Papagos were plotting to make off with his ore.

He had the girl on Begetta, armed with Walker's repeater – six shells in the magazine and one in the barrel, and cautioned to fire at the first hint of trouble.

Each time they'd stopped he'd gone around checking packs, checking the lashings, counting noses. He was over a barrel – too damned vulnerable on too many counts! That kid, if he was off on Walker's orders, might do any one of a number of things. He could be out there ahead of them setting up an ambush. He could right this minute be pacing alongside, waiting for a chance at Charlie with that pistol. He could be going for reinforcements or trying to make contact with some of Jones' scouts.

These were educated Indians with a patina

of Christian doctrine priested onto them for upwards of two hundred years, which might have stuck no better than it had with some whites exposed even longer to its gentling influence.

Point was, these Papagos understood better than most what money could do for them. They would see in this ore not only the possibility of escape from a lifetime of drudgery but a chance to strike back for all the abuses of white supremacy. And the dead called up by Walker – the "lost spirits" trapped behind rock in that mine, whose unquiet blood through all these years would have been crying for revenge – could put real fire into whatever means Walker was taking to separate these packs from their rightful owners. After all, why share when, with a pinch of risk and a dab of ingenuity, they could grab the whole works and avenge their ancient dead?

What it all amounted to from where Medders stood was that now, on top of everything else, he was faced with the very real threat of mutiny, committed to constant viligance with death the price of that first careless move.

XIX

Trouble was he couldn't divide himself up, couldn't be in more than one place at one time. And there was a choice to be made.

They were moving now through a low range of foothills, rolling and thinly stubbled with drought stunted mesquites, the greater mass of the Diablitos behind them.

Ahead lay Tubac with not much between but open flats and, beyond the river, more of the same on an upward slant to the towering slabs of the Santa Rita Mountains, reputed to shelter bands of hostile Apaches led by a local medicine man operating under the name of Geronimo. From the train's present placement to the steeps of these mountains was pretty close, Charlie judged, to being a full twenty miles, and with hardly enough cover to hide a big dog.

He passed the word for another halt to give all hands whatever rest they might snatch while he reconsidered, in the light of suspicions roused by Flores' defection, whether to make a bee line for Tubac and try to bull through by the shortest route, or drop south at once and, regardless of time and the added miles, attempt to get through the mountains by way of Sonoita Creek which, from what he recalled, looked to be both easier and considerably safer.

He was aiming, of course, for the new stamps at Charleston, recently installed by the Tombstone Mining & Milling Company. Once he had the mill's receipt they could jog over to Tombstone, pick up and cash the Company's check, get rid of the extra mules and break up. With the Weeping Widow gutted of ore, Belita, like enough, would be off to mañana land; he thought he might perhaps ride along, as far anyways as Naco. In that border town a man could thumb his nose at Jones with impunity because, if things became too uproarious, he had only to step across the line to be safe.

There was a considerable attraction to this picture of Naco, but first they would have to get the ore to Charleston and, while a dash straight through the mountains would be quickest, in the hope of cutting out a few of the risks he'd about decided to drop south and take the Sonoita Creek route when, chancing to brush against one of the waterskins, he went as suddenly still as though a diamondback rattler had reared up in his path. He stood, damp with sweat, finally reaching back a hand. That skin had scarcely ten swallows left in it!

Although, like the Papagos, he'd spent the whole night on his feet, he had not been conscious of thirst until now. His own canteen, strapped over his shoulder, was practically full, but the next waterskin he felt of was empty – and the next. With the schoolboys watching he ran to another. It was still a little clammy where the water had leaked away. The slit it had leaked from told the whole story. Too scared to curse, he was aware of time running out on him. The skins on the other mules would be empty, too, and a dehydrated mule was mighty close to being a dead one. He was minded to shoot Heap Walker out of hand.

He looked around for him and someone, a couple hundred yards nearer the front, ducked between two mules. But the girl kicked Begetta into a run and cut him off. "What is it?" she called, and Medders bitterly told her.

"Empty!" she cried. "But they can't –"

"Every last one of 'em's been slashed with a knife!" Charlie growled, hurrying up. There was no telling how many of the Papagos had been in on it, but it was near enough light that he could see Walker's

177

sneer. "Fer two cents," Medders snarled, "I'd slit his goddam throat!"

He was riled enough to, anyway. Sonoita Creek could be dry; most of the creeks had dried up in this drought. He was so filled with fury his legs were shaking.

The first flush of day was creeping over the sandy flats off ahead. Charlie knuckled the red rims of his sunken eyes. If he tried to go through those mountains with Walker they could all wind up at the bottom of some gulch. "Give him his head," he told the girl; and, to Walker: "*Git!*"

The Papago eyed Charlie's Sharps like a cornered coyote, then took off at a lope, disappearing behind a brush fringed ridge. The other three boys peered at Medders uneasily, but none felt bold enough to open his mouth. "The deal," Charlie said, "still stands, but the next whippoorwill t' lift s'much as a finger will be took care of, an' plumb permanent."

The loss of that water could turn out to be serious, no use kidding himself. Between here and Tubac, maybe three miles ahead, there was a tin-can spring, the last of his hidden water, two big cans that were going to have to be dug up and carried; and he was angrily thinking of the ore they'd have to jettison when something about the tightening

178

silence wore through his absorption to spin him, Sharps lifting, in the direction of his crew.

Against the brightening east all three stood motionless, rigid as gophers. And Charlie, twisting to follow those gray faced stares, felt his own eyes swell. He blinked, peered again, and savagely swore.

In the still morning air, back the way they had come but farther north, a spiral of smoke blackly climbed, like a finger, above the sun splashed crest of Colorado Peak.

Even as he anxiously watched, clutched by dismay, Belita's bleak cry pulled his face around to see, toward Tucson, an answering signal swirling up in quick puffs. This was coming from Twin Buttes, south and west of San Xavier, the stamping ground of Burks, hatchet man for banker Jones.

Medders blew out his cheeks in a violent fury, but could no longer doubt. Burks' scouts had a line on him and were alerting Jones' lieutenants wherever they might be, calling his understrappers into the field. The dangers were doubled. Burks' spies in the rimrocks would pick him up in two shakes if he moved onto those flats, and he was sure as hell going to have to. He had to cross the Santa Ritas or go around them, one – and

179

there was nothing but desert between him and the mountains.

"Git goin'!" he yelled, and cursed the mules into motion.

There was no help for it, and no hiding their tracks. The Sonoita Creek route was out – they couldn't risk it now. They had to have that buried water or chance the loss of every mule!

As the ore-laden mules were being rushed toward the flats Medders, shaking and swearing as though out of his mind, was trying frantically to determine what chance they had of getting into those mountains. They were twenty miles off. Whoever had sent up the first gout of smoke had to someway eat fifteen miles of back country just to come up to Charlie's present position and – since he had no intention of standing around – could be forgotten; and Twin Buttes was better than forty miles to the north, while Medders' own party would be driving straight east.

But that bunch at Twin Buttes would be well mounted, traveling light. No pack animals to slow them and the promise of cash bonuses if they ran him to earth; once they made out he was bound for those mountains they'd move diagonally to cut him off. These were obvious facts, and Burks' reputation would be spurring them hard.

And the law of this land was in Jones' pocket.

Still, Charlie thought, they just might squeak through. It was the meanest kind of country up there, much of it hidden in timber, all standing on end, cut up with gulches, sheer slabs of rock towering hundreds of feet, drops that would make a man's stomach turn over. A gamble, sure – but what had they to lose that was not lost already?

What T.K. told his sheriff would have little relation to the orders given his pet exterminator. This had gone beyond silver. Dry Camp Burks would be out for the kill. But if Medders could get his mules into those mountains they'd at least have a chance to save their lives. There was places back there where one determined man could stand off an army, so long as his shells and the grub held out.

Such plans as he could shape were filled with ifs and maybes, but inside the first hour they had reached, unearthed and sampled the hidden water, stripped one mule of its silver, dropped the packs in the pit, tramped sand over them, strapped the dug-up cans to the unpacked mule, fed each animal its bait of oats and got far enough along in their dash for the mountains to bring Tubac town near enough without glasses to be apprehensively distrustful of its abandoned appearance. Even his Papago packers looked dubious; and Belita, twisting around, called nervously: "Hadn't we better pass this place up?"

"Looks like they've had some kind of a scare," Medders growled, waving her on. "There's a well in the square – like t' be the last water we'll see this side of Charleston."

He had his eyes peeled sharp for tricks but the air of utter desertion that hung over the place, the desolate stillness of the empty square, the boarded-up windows of the store – and its open door – all spoke in silent shouts of panic flight.

Whatever it was, Charlie thought, it hadn't hit; and he was still peering around with the hairs standing stiff along the back of his neck when a Papago's shout jerked a look across his shoulder.

South of the town, and not far south at that, a new boil of smoke was raggedly rising in a churn of leaden clouds that had nothing to do with signals. That spreading, billowing, black bottomed pall, increasingly tinted with edgings of pink, spilled its screaming answer through Medders' mind. Two miles down the road the tiny Mexican hamlet of Carmen was damn well being put to the torch, and the only thing a man could get out of that was Geronimo and his Cherrycow Apaches!

He dived for the store, coming out on the run with several boxes of cartridges and three of Mr. Henry's .44-40 repeaters taking the same black-power loads as most of the hand guns generally in use, and which he passed to his packers along with instructions to water the stock – but *lightly*, for this was no time or place to be stuck with foundered animals.

While this was being taken care of and he was trying to decide if they should hole up here where at least they would have some walls to get behind, he was scouring the town in the anxious hope of coming onto some kind of overlooked transportation...like a good stout mule forgotten when these people had so hastily departed.

The livery was bare of everything but feed and harness. He ran limping around through a few more yards of tumbledown sheds, a faint but plaintive nicker brought him up with an old, nearly toothless mare. Any other time he would not have looked twice at her, but he was not right then in any mind to be choosey.

Dragging her back to the livery, anxiously

scanning that pall of black smoke, he flung an ear-stall over her roman-nosed head and, about to grab up a saddle, instead heaved a sack of oats up across her withers, and climbed aboard with a heartfelt sigh. She might not be much but she sure beat walking.

They were all waiting for him when he got back to the square, impatiently staring with scared looks at the smoke. "All right," he called, "let's git outa here." No one argued.

In less than ten minutes they were at the river, pushing through cottonwoods and spraggly willows and on across its rock and sandchoked bottom, bone dry for weeks by the look of it.

For a while, except for scattered patches of brush, the way was fairly open, as he had figured it would be; and since the rise or pitch was not as sharp as it had seemed, they were doing pretty well. But along about midmorning, with two-thirds of the jump behind, one of the boys, pointing north-east, fastened all eyes on a new outbreak of smoke. This was obviously rising from some hidden peak and was just as certainly some kind of signal. Even worse, it was rising from the very mountains they were now committed to. Still, it was a long way north, up around Greaterville someplace, and Charlie, up to his ears in more urgent worries, put it out of mind.

It was Belita, long silent, who brought into sharp focus the crux of their danger, discovering a problem in tactics which could not be got around.

The terrain had considerably changed. They were now in a region of dwarf mesquite which, practically useless as cover, was becoming increasingly hard to get through. And the ground itself was more ruggedly rising, cut up and gouged by barrancas and cutbanks channeled through the centuries by storm-water runoffs. Progress had been reduced to a snail's pace; the mules were taking ten steps to get ahead scarcely one. And it was while they were cursing their way through this that the girl, leading Begetta, discovered the horsemen barreling up on their flank.

Charlie's first thought, when she cried out, was Apaches, and he whirled to peer south across a prickling shoulder. "The other way!" Belita called.

He saw them then, perhaps five miles off but coming up at a tangent and moving at the speed of a wind-pushed cloud shadow. There looked to be about a dozen in the bunch. He couldn't be sure without a glass, but it seemed not unreasonable to assume, since they were coming from the general direction of Tucson, that this was the go-gettem outfit intrusted to Burk's – the cure-or-kill unit of the banker's organization.

He hung fire a moment, trying to estimate whether Burks could wring more out of them and, if he could, would the increase be likely to put them into the eroding detritus and blocks of fallen granite he could see poking up below the base of yonder bastions before his boys could arrive with the mules. And he could not find either for or against. Jones' understrappers, while unquestionably moving a great deal faster, had at least five extra miles to make up. Coldly, Medders knew he hadn't much choice. To try to hold them off here was plainly out of the question.

Kicking the mare into some semblance of a run, pushing past the frightened scowls of his Papagos, he grumbled at Belita, "We're gonna have t' run fer it!" and put the mare, on her haunches, down a slope of sliding shale.

This wasn't what he wanted, but it was going to have to do. He was going to have to trust the girl to keep the animals bunched and moving. This arroyo he'd dropped into was cluttered with brush and boulders that would slow them further and, because of its tangent, would fetch them to the base of those towering cliffs a good ways off from the spot he had chosen, but at least it would keep them hidden from Burks.

There was no predicting what his Papagos would do, now he'd armed them; he could only hope Belita and their fright would keep them in line.

The arroyo petered out a hundred yards from cliffs that looked, when he came out of it, to be not only unbroken but too sheer even for a goat to find a foot hold. In this exposed position he twisted around to look for Burks and his hardcases, churning up quite a splatter of electrifying hope when they were not at once apparent. But this relief was short lived; they were out there, all right. They came surging abruptly from a gully scarce a rifleshot away, and the whistling *whang-g-g* of a ricochet screaming Charlie's name as it tore off past his elbow very amply described the pitch of their temper.

He flung himself from the mare like a ruptured duck and, as the first of the mules came panting into the open, went scuttling with his Sharps for the nearest rock – seeing, even as he did so, the sun skittering off the wicked drive of raked spurs.

From the corners of his stare he got an impression of more mules bounding white-eyed past in snorting flight toward the cliffs. *"Keep 'em goin'!"* he yelled at the girl's frightened face, and brought the buffalo gun to his shoulder, feeling the recoil in every muscle of his body.

Through the blackpowder smoke he saw two outflung arms and a man reeling off the back of his horse. With no time for adjusting the sight he fired again, holding lower to compensate, seeing a second man pitch from the saddle as the rest sheered off to hunt cover like rabbits. And he was up and running himself on the instant, putting into it every ounce of drive he could summon, to fall wheezing behind the rotten rock of an outcrop some good forty yards nearer the base of the cliffs.

Blood pounding in his ears, he couldn't hear for the bedlam of enraged shouts and gunfire as Burks' dismounted scalp hunters tried to blast him off the face of the earth. Rock chips struck like hail around him as he lay squeezed flat against the stony ground.

XX

We are told uncounted times how a man, faced with death, knows regret for past mistakes as in those last fleeting moments forgotten faces in flying sequence flash across the stricken mind.

It was not that way with Medders.

Though between a rock and the devil's own doorstep, crammed with the bitterness of frustrated hate – scared to move and even more afraid not to – the only thing he was regretting right then was that he could not take a lot more of them with him. Particularly Burks.

Behind him the mules had all passed out of sight; the only things to be seen back there was cliffs, fallen rock and sunbaked shale. He had never felt so alone in his life.

He could twist his head but dared move nothing else. Most of the noise had dropped away till there was just enough firing to keep him pinned down while his thoughts cringed and snarled at imagined activities given cold credence by sundry scrapings and scufflings, the occasional clatter of disturbed stones.

To lift his head up to where he might see was almost certain to summon that last blue whistler, and if he didn't look soon that bunch would be all over him. He had cut his twine too short for this play; and just as he was snapping the lever on another 525-grain bullet, gathering his muscles to come up shooting, the sudden slam of two rifles barking viciously back of him changed the whole look of everything.

Convinced he'd run his string plumb out, relief rushing through him almost turned him dizzy when one of Burks' scalp hunters let out a cry and several booted pairs of nearby feet broke simultaneously into a frantically departing dash for cover.

Charlie, lunging erect, knocked one of them sprawling, and was fumbling to thumb a fresh load into the breech when the girl's jumpety voice cried: "Back here – *hurry!*"

Still crammed with the spleen of un-appeared anger, belligerent and reckless with strain and resentment, he would have stayed to shoot more except that all who were able had ducked out of sight.

Disgusted, he finally limped toward Belita who, with one of the boys, was still banging away. "Put some whack in it," she snapped. "We can't hold them forever!"

In the nest of rocks they had his caught

190

mare waiting and from there he could see the narrow slot in the cinnamon cliffs through which the mules had been driven. The girl, pointing toward it as he climbed onto the mare, said, "It opens into a canyon about a quarter mile back."

"We better hope," Medders grunted, "it don't turn out t' be a *box.*"

They caught up with the mules and the other two schoolboys about a mile farther on and Medders knew inside the next quarter hour that if this gulch dead-ended they would have no recourse but to fight their way out, which – considering the odds if Burks' bunch forted up – was no salubrious prospect.

And, sure enough, the damned walls darkly towering above them commenced with alarming suddenness to close up, pinching in until Eddie Two-Cow, up at the front, had a hard time keeping them off his elbows. The girl kept peering anxiously at Medders and Charlie, bull stubborn, kept waving them on. To go back, in his opinion, was no better than plain suicide and, anyway, this crevice had grown so narrow there wasn't room to turn around. His two-legged animals could probably manage and maybe even the burro, but not those mules.

The cant of the ground grew rougher and

steeper, and more and more often became all but closed off with rock chunks dropped from the rotten rims which had to be scrambled over. If one of the animals broke a leg in the process. . . .

He refused to follow so repugnant a thought; the things he *had* to look at held all the grief one man could stomach.

The rock strewn bed of this twisting crevice led the clatter of hoofs and these mute, stumbling humans ever higher and deeper into the stone ribbed flank of the mountain, the walls climbing with them toward a blue crack of sky which seemed presently as remote as the likelihood of getting the ore through to Charleston.

Though he frequently looked back, expecting each time to find Burks plunging after them, he was more fiercely concerned lest this tortuous passage either pinch out completely or become impassably choked. If it narrowed another five inches they would have no choice but to abandon the ore – at least the bigger part of it, and he was not even sure they would be *able* to.

Where, for instance, could they put it?

Not in their pockets. And if they dumped it onto this ribbon of ground how – cramped as they were, traveling head to tail – would any but the first be able to get past? Sure,

Medders thought bitterly, the girl, the Papagos and himself could manage to scramble over it no doubt – but never those mules!

Though he had not yet caught a glimpse of Burks or any sign Jones' kill crew was back of them, he could not believe a pistolero of Dry Camp's vanity and grudge-ridden pertinacity would ever willingly give over with the end so close to his hate-bared choppers. The guy was simply playing it cautious, waiting for Charlie to trap himself for them or get into some bind where it would be just the same as shooting fish in a barrel. That was Burks every time – he got paid for scalps, not for taking crazy chances!

And there was another wicked hunch breathing down Charlie's neck, a nasty premonition that he may have been out-figured. When you counted the resources at Jones' disposal, all the bonus hunting men he'd put into the field, you couldn't hardly feel it likely the banker any longer would have much doubt of their destination.

And then, abruptly, the worst of Charlie's fears came home to roost. Unable to gauge how far or high they had come – except that the walls hanging over him seemed lower – Medders rounded another of the crack's sharp twists and found the whole train stopped.

It wasn't the end of the road, but it might just as well have been, he guessed in the bitterness of consternation. Ahead of them the passage stretched out, ironically, straight as an arrow and, within five hundred yards, climbed into the sunswept windy open – just five hundred goddam yards, Medders thought.

To be licked, that near, by forty feet of fallen rock!

But there it was, jammed tight, forty feet of piled-up rubble, jagged chunks sticking out that nothing short of dynamite could move in a month of Sundays! There was no possibility of taking the mules over this – they couldn't even be turned around. There was nothing, by God, he could do but shoot them. Mare and mules! It damn near made him cry.

He put Belita with Walker's rifle around the bend to watch for Burks. The rest of them, sweating like pigs, went to work. He gave the last of their water in his hat to Begetta and then, the boys helping, man-handled her bodily over the worst spots while the mules stood patiently waiting their turn. Charlie groaned, as in fever, but they were too big to handle.

It took an hour and twenty minutes to get the burro past that jumble of wedged-in broken sections of rimrock, to retrieve a pack saddle and as much of the ore as he dared risk putting on her. Long before they were finished Belita's rifle cracked twice, filling the gorge with a bedlam of echoes. Charlie sent one of the Papagos back to help her keep Burks pinned down, glad that the bend concealed their reason for having stopped. Had Burks known their predicament he might have talked his toughs into making an all-out effort. As it was – faced as it seemed with determined resistance – he could tell himself there was nothing to be gained that could not be taken care of easier and cheaper in the dark of the moon. At least Medders hoped that was how Dry Camp would see it.

When they were ready he slipped back and with a hand-sign called in the girl and Papago. Just as they were about to squeeze past the mules he said, keeping his voice down: "Any ore you wanta take along in yer clothes you can keep without dividin', but it'll sure git heavier with every mile you lug it."

"Thanks for nothing," Belita said, grimacing, and squirmed on by without so much as a look. Medders stepped aside to let the schoolboy through, but education got the best of Eddie. He stopped by the last split-open pack, fastened his pantslegs tight at the ankles, unloosened his belt and filled both sides to bulging. He put several of the smaller chunks inside his shirt and finally jammed three more up under his hat.

Medders got the Sharps, slung his canteen over a shoulder, and followed. The boy was making rough work of the rockpile. Belita was just scrambling down the far side when Medders, relieving Eddie Two-Cow of his Henry repeater, let go a deep sigh and started shooting mules.

It made a hellish racket, and when he was done he smashed the wooden stock and bent the barrel out of shape before flinging it away from him. This didn't make him feel any better but it was something he could do. He caught up with Eddie, helped him down off the rocks and then, still looking like hell warmed over, struck off after the others. He glanced back once, halfway to the crest, and discovered Eddie Two-Cow throwing away some of the ore he had stuffed in his pantslegs.

The others, with Begetta, stood waiting at the summit, and he was just coming up with them when a rattle of rifleshots jerked him around, to find Eddie staggering into a run, to see him knocked off his feet with his mouth stretched wide in a yell that never came, and Burks' bunch back of him swarming onto the rock ham. He pulled the Sharps' sight up as far as it would go, clapped the stock to his shoulder and hauled back on the trigger.

The solid boom of that buffalo gun cut through lesser sounds like the crash of a cannon. One of Burks' rannies went down as though swept from his knees by a scythe. Crazily Medders stood pouring lead into them, firing as fast as he could cram in the shells. One fellow spun, taking another guy with him. One, almost clear, fell with both arms flopping.

When Charlie, still fuming, came up with Belita, the girl said: "Is that it?"

The whole world, it seemed like, was spread out below them. Following her look Charlie, glowering, nodded. It was not so terrible far as the crow flew but the way they would have to go, hoofing each mile with their loss and anxieties, Charleston seemed almost at the ends of the earth.

Notwithstanding the bitter thoughts they kept chewing, parched throats, burning feet, empty bellies and the constant worry of running into Apaches, at just a fraction past nine of the following morning Medders, sourly waving his paper to dry off the ink, stepped from the office of the T.M. & M. full into the smash of the climbing sun to suddenly stop as though hit by a mallet.

Equally stunned, the others stopped back of him to stand anxiously peering into the fat shaved-hog face of Tiberius Jones and his gaunt-shouldered sheriff.

Bad enough it had been to get scarcely more for the ore on Begetta than half what he'd got from O'Toole back in Tucson. Break this into four shares, he'd disgustedly thought, and it would just about manage to take care of his chewing. And now to be caught flat-footed, check still in hand, put such a strain on the clutch of his temper that if he'd been packing a pistol he'd probably have grabbed it. He hadn't even a pocket knife and his Sharps, belatedly remembered, was still in the office, uselessly leaning where he'd set it against the damned counter.

McFarron, recalling perhaps better days when they'd been cronies, shifted and, scowling, started to open his mouth. But Jones, staring hard at the check, waved back his sheriff.

Breaking through the tight fit of his Judas smile the great man said like an elder brother: "All right – you win. I'm a big

198

enough sport to own up when I'm beat. Put a reasonable price on that mine and I'll buy it."

Charlie almost choked. But the banker, misreading him and quick to seize any sign of an advantage, declared like Moses handing down the great stones: "I'll give you one hundred thousand, sight unseen – that's fair enough, isn't it?"

"It ain't a question of fair –"

"Make it a hundred and fifty," Belita said, "and you've got it."

Charlie glared at her; Jones, peering at both of them, switched his attention to the girl. Caught between caution and greed he said carefully. "I'd have to go out there, you know ... I've got to be able to find it again."

"These boys here can show you," Belita smiled, watching Charlie. "They know where it is – they helped us pack in that ore. Put a cashier's check in my hand and it's yours."

Charlie looked apoplectic. "Here, wait –"

Jones said: "It's a deal!"